THE ADVENTURES
OF
AMPHI-BOY
AND
HIS FRIENDS

H. V. FERNANDES SR.

Order this book online at www.trafford.com
or email orders@trafford.com

Most Trafford titles are also available at major online book retailers.

Printed in the United States of America.

ISBN: 978-1-4669-2059-0 (sc)
ISBN: 978-1-4669-2058-3 (e)

Trafford rev. 03/23/2012

 www.trafford.com

North America & international
toll-free: 1 888 232 4444 (USA & Canada)
phone: 250 383 6864 ♦ fax: 812 355 4082

CONTENTS

This book is dedicated to:

My wife Sharon
And my grandson
Eric Daniel Ramsay

PROLOGUE

This is a story garnered from the writings of an 11 year old boy with a vivid imagination. The 11 year old boy is my grandson Eric Daniel Ramsay and his story is as follows. Written exactly as he wrote it. Remember this is an 11 year old writing.

CHAPTER 1

MERMAN

Bang, Smash, the Water and Lightning.
There's a family of four, the dad, the boy, Jamie, the mom and the sister Sarah. Jamie and his dad rented a boat and got a crew and set off to a sea in Wyoming Spring water. After 2 days on the sea there was a big lightning storm and the boat was rocking side to side and then bang, lightning hit's the boat and blows it up. Everybody dies except Jamie. He manages to hang on until a board hits Jamie on the head and knocks him out and falls to the bottom of the ocean. Jamie wakes up and starts to breathe. "How am I breathing?" You have a gift from the water Goddess. "Who said that?" Me, I am going to be your trainer. "OK if your going to be my trainer then show yourself and tell me your name" My name is Link Sasque. "Ok Link Sasque" call me Link "Ok Link why and how am I breathing under water?" You got gills on your neck, they are gifts from the water Goddess. Ok you said that you are my trainer. Yes I am going to teach you your powers.

THE NEW POWER THE STUN

"Ok Link bring me to the station" What station we don't have a training station said Link. You mean I have to learn the hard way.

Yup. We have to get the power star back. The pencil heads stole it.

They have a guard at every gate to get inside the pencil heads village.

Ok there going to be sharks in the seaweed so that's where your going to be practicing stunning. "That's going to be my first power?" Yes. "Ok where is the pencil head village?" Long way from here. Do you have like sea horses and a car or something? Nope. So were suppost to swim. No that's where magic comes in I'm only going halfway so I can practice my power" Ok how about going to that seaweed and concentrating on a blue beam than close your eyes. Remember concentrate on a blue beam.

Jamie stunned Link before he could finish his sentence. "Ok how am I suppost to unstun" Smash! You don't the stun goes away after a couple minutes. It looks like I'm going to have to teach you the undo spell. "Ok I'm going to learn a new spell now."

CHAPTER 3

PENCIL HEADS CASTLE

After 2 days of training they get to the pencil heads village. Ok were at the first gate to get in you know how to deal with these guys said Link. "I do? I mean I do." concentrate on that blue beam then close your eyes said Link "Okay I know how to do this Zap Jamie stuned his first enemy. Now go through the gate and stun some more pencil heads! Yeah let's go! Charge yell with me Link charge, Link where did you go. Link! Look like I'm going to have to get the star by myself here I go."

A couple minutes later Jamie's in an ice cage in the pencil heads castle. "How am I suppost to get out of here? I've been in here for four days there's no way out of here. Who said that" I did my name is Carbs I thought I was the only merman. There's only one way out.

That is all he wrote and I took up the story line and wrote this book. I hope you enjoy it as much as I enjoyed writing it.

THE ADVENTURES OF
AMPHI-BOY
AND HIS FRIENDS

CHAPTER 1

THE EXPLOSION

A family of four, who live in Wyoming, decides to take a vacation in Florida. Mainly because they wanted to see and enjoy the ocean. The family consists of a mom and dad whose ages we won't discuss; their 14 year old son, Jamie; and their 10 year old daughter, Sarah.

Wyoming, being mountainous and in the Mid West, doesn't have a lot of water to go boating in. Big water that is. They were a long ways from either ocean and had always talked of and planned on taking a vacation in Florida. Where they heard the water was always warm and clear. So now, after scrimping and saving for the past year, here they were, in a little place not far from Miami.

They were enjoying the sun on the beach outside of the cabin they had rented for the two weeks they planned on being there. Mom and dad were sitting in lounge chairs soaking up the sun. Jamie was spending most of his time in the water and now was casually swimming up and down the beach in front of some hot looking babes in bikinis. The girls were pretending not to see him, which made Jamie start to show off. He would dive under the water, go down to the bottom and suddenly shoot up high out of the water and make a big splash coming down. This in turn made the girls giggle and start to take notice of him, which made him do it again and again. At the same time taking him closer to the girls.

His sister Sarah, noticing the girls looking at him, got a little jealous and started yelling to him saying:

"Jamie! JAMIE!! Help me build a sand castle . . . . PLEASE?" she added.

"Not now Sis." he yelled back. "Later." He also added.

The girls had been starting to walk towards him but now they stopped. Looking from Jamie to his sister then back to Jamie. They shrugged their shoulders and said:

"We don't really care for guys who won't help their sister when she asks them to." With that they quickly walked further down the beach, away from Jamie.

Jamie slaps the water, probably really wanting to slap his sister, but says:

"Oh, alright. Lets build a sand castle."

The two of them huddle down in the sand and proceed to build what kind of looks like a castle. But you have to have a big imagination to see it. They spent the rest of the day building and rebuilding the castle 'till the tide came in and washed everything away. It was starting to get late so they all went back to the cabin and, after a day in the sun and in the water, they were soon snuggled up in their beds sound asleep.

The next morning, after breakfast, they went back out to the beach. Again they were in and out of the water and playing water tag and dodgem with the beach ball. Jamie noticed that there were boat rental places all up and down the beach. So he runs to his dad and says:

"Can we rent a boat and go out to sea?"

His dad says. "Maybe. Lets go ask your mom."

So they hustle off to find his mom and sister and find them busy playing with a couple of crabs in some rocks along the upper edge of the beach.

"Hey honey," his dad says, "Lets rent a boat and go out in the ocean for a while." He didn't tell her it was Jamie's idea.

"We don't know how to handle a boat!" she exclaims.

"We can hire a couple of guys who do. That way we won't have to worry about handling the boat and just relax and have fun." He tells her.

"Come on mom," Sarah says, "It'll probably be more exciting than playing with crabs."

"Oh. Alright. It most likely will be more fun than this." She says.

"But not out of sight of land." she adds.

So Jamie and his dad go to one of the rental places and rent a good size boat and a couple of men to handle it. The four of them (six counting the two man crew) set out to sea off the coast of Florida. There are many uncharted little islands just off the coast. Before heading out too far they stop at several of these islands. Jamie and his dad are doing a lot of snorkeling and kind of fooling around splashing each other. Sarah and her mom are collecting sand dollars and all kinds of sea shells that have washed up on the shore of the island.

After stopping at about the fourth or fifth island, and doing the same things Jamie is starting to get bored and restless. He turns to his dad and says:

"Hey Dad! Why don't we go out further and find an island that is more deserted than these?"

Many other boaters were stopping here also and it was getting kind of crowded.

"I want us to be like the Robinson Crusoe family, and we can build a shack and do some spear fishing, and live off the land."

His dad laughs and says: "I don't know son, how long do you think we're going to be out here anyway?"

"Long enough to build a shack at least." says Jamie.

"Come on please? Just for a while." he begs.

"Let's see what your mother says." His dad replies, and heads off to talk to Jamie's mom. It takes him a little while to get her to agree, all the time Jamie is pacing the beach and acting like he's praying to a god above. His father returns and says:

"Okay, but we're not going too far out. Remember what your mom said, 'not out of sight of land'. A few hours out and that's it. If we don't find an island by then, we're coming back in. Okay?" his father says.

"Okay." whoops Jamie and he quickly runs down the beach and hurries his sister back to the boat with her protesting all the way.

"My shells!" She exclaims, "I've got to get my shells!" she screams!

"I'll get them." Jamie yells back at her. So Jamie jumps on board the boat and gets a plastic bag and runs over and collects her shells in it and brings them on board, almost throwing them at her.

"Here's your precious shells." he says.

"We'll get some more on the deserted island we land on," he adds, "and they'll probably be better ones than these."

After his mom climbs back aboard, they proceed to go further out looking for this deserted island Jamie wants to see.

Jamie has a very rich and fancy imagination and always wanted to be an adventurer. He fancies himself as being a modern day buccaneer. Of being the top banana on an island all his own and lording it over other castaways. Of searching for and finding treasures consisting of pearls, emeralds and diamonds. His imagination has no end to it.

They stop in The Grand Bahamas for awhile and buy some mementos to take back with them, but needless to say The Grand Bahamas aren't deserted islands. Jamie keeps reminding his parents of this and is anxious to continue looking for the deserted island he hopes to find. Upon leaving the Bahamas, they continue traveling straight out to sea. They had neglected to get a map of the ocean and the islands, so they were traveling by compass only and guesswork. This kind of made Jamie's dad think that maybe these two men he hired weren't such good sailors after all. Why didn't they think of getting a map? Of course if it is a deserted island, it wouldn't be on any map, is what Jamie thinks.

After going about two hundred miles out in the ocean, and out of sight of land. Mom hadn't noticed this because she and Sarah were sunbathing on the floor of the boat. Jamie's dad was busy fishing, without any luck and Jamie was hanging off the bow of the boat, yelling "yo ho ho". They weren't finding a deserted island. So they decide to head back towards land, even though Jamie was begging to continue to go further.

"Just a little farther out," he pleads.

"There's bound to be an island somewhere close," he cries.

They hadn't noticed the skies darkening up behind them when they were heading out to sea. His father, looking back now, sees that the skies are dark and looking very scary.

"We have to head back now and quick!" He exclaims.

"Let's hope we can get back before the storm hits us." He yells, as the wind is suddenly picking up.

"Turn this boat around and let's get out of here!" He yells to the deck hands that were supposed to be guiding them. It seems that they were so wrapped up with watching Jamie's antics that they hadn't noticed the change in the weather either.

Or they were just not good deck hands to begin with and had lied to Jamie's dad just to get some money. Now they hoped to get back to land before it stated storming.

Suddenly a lightning bolt comes crashing down with a crack that is deafening, making them all jump as if they had been shot, letting them know that it was to late now. The clouds open up and release all their water, as if someone had opened up a faucet, which soaks them instantly. The storm is upon them in all its fury. Streaks of lightning are flashing all around them and the thunder keeps crashing almost constantly. Being so far from any sign of land, they have to ride it out the best they can.

Mom and Sarah quickly go below deck screaming. They are terrified and huddle together in the bunk sobbing. With each crack of thunder they scream and hug each other even tighter.

Dad goes below deck also, to try to comfort and assure them that everything will be alright. If truth be told, he was just about as terrified as they were, and wasn't sure they would be alright. He had to put on a brave act for their sakes though. He was trusting the seamanship of the two men he had hired to pull them through this. Jamie, being a curious and brave boy, (thinking he was brave anyway), and acting the part of a buccaneer and a fool, is up on deck and holding on for dear life in the bow of the boat, where the storm has caught him.

Long streaks of lightning light up the sky and silhouette the boat against the rolling sea. Giant waves come crashing across the boat as if trying to wash him off. With each crashing wave he would hang on tight and afterwards yell:

"IS THAT ALL YOU'VE GOT?" Shaking a fist in the air after wiping his face clear of sea water.

"YOU'VE GOTTA DO BETTER THAN THAT TO GET ME." He screams, quickly getting a tight grip on the railing he was clinging to with both hands, as the next wave comes pouring over him.

"JAMIE! JAMIE!" His father is yelling, "YOU NEED TO BE DOWN HERE WITH US."

But with the howling of the wind and the crashing of the waves, and the deafening thunder, Jamie can't hear him. He would probably be washed or pitched overboard if he does try to go to the cabin door anyway. The boat is rocking and pitching something fierce, from side to side, up and down, riding the waves as if being just as defiant as Jamie. One minute it would be on top of the waves and the next minute almost under the waves. It came close to capsizing about umpteen times already.

These waves have got to be at least twenty feet high.

Just as his father is about to go up and get him, **BANG!!!**, lightning hits the boat and blows it up. Mom, dad, and Sarah die instantly in the explosion along with the crew. But Jamie, because he was in the bow of the boat, is thrown in the water.

There is nothing but pieces left of the boat. Jamie, who is now really scared and completely lost, manages to hang on to a floating piece of a seat. Treading water and looking around, he can see nothing. No boat!! Nothing!! Just a lot of pieces floating around him. So thorough and devastating was the explosion.

The storm continues to rage, as if saying:

"THIS IS WHAT I'VE GOT LITTLE BOY, NOW DEAL WITH IT."

"DAD!!! MOM!!!" Jamie screams. "WHERE ARE YOU??"

"S A R A H!!...D A D D Y!!...M O M M Y!!" He screams again and again still clinging to the seat. This continues for what seems like hours, but in reality is only about ten or maybe fifteen minutes. Then a huge wave comes crashing down on him, making him lose his grip on the seat, and completely engulfing him in its grasp. Jamie is pushed down deep beneath the surface. As he is struggling to reach the surface a piece of board hits him in the head with such force that it knocks him out and the last thing Jamie remembers, is trying to get to the surface and getting some air into his lungs.

Jamie sinks, ever so slowly,
down,
down,
down,
down,
to the bottom of the ocean, like a leaf, falling from a tree.

THE CHANGE

J amie wakes up and is very confused and his head hurts. He doesn't remember being in the boat, or the storm, or the explosion. He can't seem to focus his eyes too clearly. Everything seems to be a blur. He rubs his eyes to try to clear them, but things are still hazy and looks like he's in a fog. Not knowing where he is, he tries to stand up. Being in the water, he sort of floats upward as he stands. He flaps his arms to stay upright.

"Hey!" he wonders out loud, "I'm in water! Where am I? How am I breathing?" He brings his hands up in front of his face and pushes outward, causing him to move backward in the water.

"NO! NO!" He says again out loud.

"This is impossible! Am I dead? Did I drown? Is this what happens to people who drown??? If I'm dead, how come I'm still breathing??"

Hearing himself talking, he wonders; how can I hear, talk and breathe under water? This time not talking out loud.

"You have a gift from the water goddess, Ameena." says a voice very clearly from out of the murky waters nearby.

Startled Jamie tries to whirl around to see who spoke only to float to the side and slightly upward. Steadying himself once again by flapping his arms wildly, Jamie cries in alarm:

"WHO SAID THAT?" still flapping his arms frantically, for he is very unsteady on his feet, not being used to standing on the ocean bottom. He is more floating then standing though and he has to lean against the current to stay in one spot. He is now totally scared and about to go out of his mind and freak out.

"Me, I am going to be your trainer." said the voice.

Jamie could tell he was laughing at him by the sound of his voice.

"Don't worry you'll get used to moving around down here after you get your bearings." He assures Jamie, still laughing.

"My bearings? You mean my sea legs don't you?" Jamie retorts boldly, trying hard not to be scared and thinking he can scare whoever or whatever this may be that is talking to him.

"Oh boy. I see you still have a sense of humor." the voice continues.

"That is good because you will need it to be able to handle what is in store for you." The voice says.

"WHERE ARE YOU? LET ME SEE YOU!" Jamie shouts.

"IF YOUR GOING TO BE MY TRAINER, THEN SHOW YOURSELF AND TELL ME YOUR NAME!" Jamie is trying to sound tough, and still trying to stand still without having to flap his arms to stay upright. He is yelling because he's scared.

"No need to yell . . . My name is Link Sasque." says the voice, and a kind of funny little creature, about three foot tall and looking sort of like a turtle, comes out of the weeds about fifteen or sixteen feet in front of Jamie. It is walking on its hind legs like a man. It has fins on its back and two long antennas sticking out from just over his eyes. Instead of claws on its feet it has four toes with webbing in between them at the end of its short, dumpy legs that disappear into its shell-like body. Its arms are also short and scaly with fins coming out up to its elbows. Its hands have only three fingers on them and also has webbing. It has a tail that's about two feet long and stiff with what looks like two inch barbs coming out along its length. It has long flowing dark brown hair with traces of grey in it. Jamie can't tell if it is a male or a female.

This time it's Jamie who starts laughing and doesn't try to hide it either. Its hair seems to be waving constantly as though it was floating in water. Jamie thinks to himself then exclaims: "WAIT A MINUTE!!! . . . IT IS FLOATING IN WATER!! I'M IN WATER!!! AND THIS IS REALLY HAPPENING!!!" Jamie yells excitedly. His laughter quickly disappears. But, after seeing this funny and comical creature, Jamie suddenly feels superior and although he still can't seem to stand in one place too good, he says in a rough way;

"Okay Link Sasque!" Jamie says, trying to calm down.

"Call me Link." The creature interrupts calmly and quietly.

"What?" Jamie asks, thinking of what he's going to say.

"I said call me Link." the creature says.

"Okay Link! Why and how am I breathing under water? And how can I talk and hear you? And how can I stand still like you are? And how am I able to stay down here without rising to the surface?" Jamie asks kind of loud and not very nice. (Ever try to stay down on the bottom when you go swimming? It's really impossible. Try it next time your at the beach.)

Link sighs deeply and pointing at Jamie's neck, says:

"I already told you. it's a gift from the water Goddess Ameena. Her magic keeps you down here and you've got gills on your neck just under your jawbone."

Jamie quickly feels his neck and a surprised look comes on his face as he feels the gills. His eyes get really wide and his mouth drops open. He runs his fingers over them very gently as they seem to be soft and delicate. They also seem to be pulsing with every breath he takes or thinks he's taking, as he's not breathing air, but actually taking in water through his mouth. Oxygen is going to his lungs while the water is going out his gills after going down through his stomach and up again. He can actually feel the water coming out of the gills. It feels warmer than the water around him, actually, the water around him doesn't feel cold either. He feels as though he was in a swimming pool.

"They are what makes you able to breathe in water and take the oxygen out of it." says Link patiently and calmly.

"How else do you think you would be breathing?" Link asks.

"You would drown if you were using your lungs the normal human way." He states.

"And another thing, you think you are talking with your mouth, but you are really communicating telepathically and so am I. Notice that my mouth isn't moving when you hear me talking." He says, touching his lips with his finger.

Jamie was indeed watching his mouth and was amazed to see that it wasn't moving like he said. This, however, doesn't do much to calm him. He still moves his mouth when talking. As a matter of fact, as already mentioned, he is actually breathing through his mouth and doesn't even realize this. He no longer breathes through his nose for it leads directly to his lungs and he would drown if he tried to breathe through his nose. So, without knowing that he is doing it, his mouth is moving constantly like a fishes mouth, taking in water, in order for him to breathe.

"Okay that tells me how I'm breathing and . . . . uh, ... communicating but how did I get here? Why am I given this gift?" All of a sudden a look of wonder comes over his face, then fear. He is remembering what happened.

"I was on a boat . . . . We were looking for an island . . . . A storm came up . . . . The boat blew up!" Turning toward Link and trying to grab him, he says:

"WHERE IS MY FAMILY? . . . ARE THEY ALRIGHT? . . . ARE THEY LIKE ME TOO? . . . TALK TO ME!!" Jamie is yelling and stumbling around trying to grab Link who is dodging him.

"Whoa! Whoa! Take it easy! I'm trying to help you." Link says still dodging Jamie. Which isn't hard for him to do as Jamie is very awkward and clumsy seeing as he is not used to being in water.

"Your family didn't make it." Link says, without thinking of what this would do to Jamie.

"WHAT?" Jamie says, and stops in his tracks, that is if he made any tracks. "WHAT DID YOU SAY?"

"I am very sorry about your family and crew. They were killed instantly in the explosion and the Goddess Ameena could not help them . . . . They didn't suffer," he adds quickly as he sees Jamie jerk suddenly and violently, and he begins shaking really hard.

He sinks to the sandy bottom and lays outstretched on his stomach pounding the bottom with his fists. Which makes him appear to bounce off the bottom up and down with each strike of his fists.

"IT WAS MY FAULT!" he cries out loudly.

"I WANTED TO FIND A DESERTED ISLAND, THAT'S WHY WE WERE OUT THERE SO FAR FROM LAND." he cries still banging on the ground.

Link doesn't know what to make of this. He'd never seen anyone so upset before, let alone a human. Sea creatures don't ordinarily get close to one another because their lives can end suddenly. They either get caught by fishermen or eaten by other sea creatures and even may be eaten by a member of their own family. Mothers, fathers, sisters, brothers, it doesn't make a difference to sea creatures. Some of them don't even know their mothers or fathers, or sisters or brothers When they disappear no-one cares or misses them. They are hatched from eggs long after their parents made and laid them. That's why he came out so matter of factually telling Jamie that his family didn't make it. Not knowing what to do he just stands there for a few moments watching Jamie pound the ground and bouncing around. Then says:

"They never felt a thing. As the explosion was right under them." Link says in a louder voice than normal . . . normal for him anyway. This news made Jamie stop shaking and pounding the ground, but not stop crying.

"HOW DO YOU KNOW THAT? (sob) YOU WEREN'T THERE! (sob)" Jamie yells in between crying loudly.

"The Goddess Ameena told me, when she instructed me to help you." Link says.

The tears Jamie was shedding were being swallowed up by the water surrounding him so Link did not notice them. To Link it appeared that Jamie was just making a lot of funny faces, and he continued on . . . again loudly:

"I am going to train you in the use of your new powers." he says quickly, hoping to get Jamie's attention on him.

This made Jamie stop crying and brushing his eyes as if wiping the tears away, he sits up and asks;

"POWERS?? . . . . What POWERS?? . . . . I have POWERS??" He asks calming down now and slowly rising to his feet or floating to his feet you might say.

Relieved that Jamie quieted down and didn't push for more details, Link sighs deeply again and says:

"Yes you do, or will have shortly, and I am going to teach you how to use them so you can help us."

"HELP you! Help YOU!! I mean, how can I help you when you have a Goddess. One who can give me gills and make me breathe under water . . . and . . . and . . . practically make me a fish?" Inquires Jamie in amazement.

"That's what I'm going to teach you. There are some things we have to do for ourselves without the help of the Goddess." replies Link, in explanation.

"Oh yeah! . . . . Like what?" Asks Jamie suspiciously.

"Like staying alive for one thing." Replies Link.

"There are a lot of perils down here in the deep, not just from other sea creatures but from humans too . . . . and from the sea itself." Link informs him.

"But before I can teach you anything I need to know your name. I can't just say, 'hey you', every time I want to say something to you. What is your name?" he asks.

"My name is Jamie . . . Jamie Johnson." replies Jamie.

Link responds, "Jamie? . . . . Johnson? No that's not a good name for you down here. I think we should call you something more appropriate for what you have now become. Let me see . . . . ah . . . yes Amphi-boy! Yeah, Amphi-boy that sounds good."

"AMPHI-BOY!!" exclaims Jamie. "Why Amphi-boy?" he asks a bit more lower than yelling.

"Amphi from Greek, meaning two or both. Which you are now, both fish and human. Gills and Lungs." Link explains.

"You are now a merman . . . Uh more like a merboy, but there are other mermen down here so you will be known as Amphi-boy from now on. Amphi for short, okay?" Link adds.

"Amphi-boy??? Amphi!! Yeah that sounds cool," says Jamie who is now "Amphi", and is now starting to get with the program. He leans forward into the current, swaying gently back and forth, still flapping his arms.

"It rolls smoothly off the tongue and begins with the letter A which is the first letter of our alphabet and this is my first time being a merman. Okay Link, I'm Amphi-boy from now on." He agrees.

"Amphi for short." He adds, again agreeing with Link.

Link again sighs deeply for the third time, glad that this is all settled, he's tired of sighing.

"Now are you ready to begin your training Amphi?" he asks.

"No, not until you tell me how to stop my swaying and flapping my arms like an idiot. How come you can stand still and I can't?" Amphi complains.

"Be patient, all in good time." Link says smiling at his difficulty at standing, this time without sighing.

"The Goddess Ameena will handle that part of your training," he adds in explanation.

"You keep saying the Goddess Ameena . . . The Goddess Ameena. When am I going to meet her? . . . . Seeing as she did this to me . . . Why isn't she here? How come she doesn't want to face me so I can tell her what I think?" Jamie asks defiantly.

Link only smiles and chuckling he says:

"All in good time my friend . . . . All in good time. Are we ready now?"

CHAPTER 3

THE STUN

"Alright then, bring me to the station Link Sasque" Amphi says.

"Station!! What station?" Link inquires looking around, thinking he must have missed something.

"The training station of course." Says Amphi.

"What do you mean training station?" says Link.

"You know. Where you're going to train me!" Amphi says, in a kind of exasperated way.

"Oh 'that' station. Well I guess we're in the training station then, because you're going to train right here," responds Link.

"You mean I have to learn here? Even though I can't stand still here?" Amphi exclaims in amazement.

For the first time since regaining consciousness he starts looking around to see exactly where he is and what is around him. He sees nothing but sand and rocks ahead of him. Looking behind him he sees the weeds that Link had come out of and they look pretty solid, almost like a wall.

"Yes you do, and don't worry about standing still, that'll be the least of your worries." Link replies with a wide grin on his face. Then he turns serious.

"We have to get the power star back from the Pencil Heads who stole it and took it to their castle. They have a guard at every gate to get inside their castle so it'll be very difficult to get in and get it back."

"Power star!! Pencil Heads!! Castle!! What are you talking about?" asks Jamie puzzled and raising his brows.

"The power star is a green, star shaped, magic gem that powers King Neptune's Trident. And we have to get it back soon, as his Trident is getting low and needs recharging." Link explains.

"If the Pencil Heads figure out how to use it we will all be in trouble. Including the surface dwelling people," he adds.

"Again with the Pencil Heads? Who are they? . . . . And why do you call them Pencil Heads?" asks Amphi.

Link says, "They are our enemies and the enemy of most all of the denizens of the deep. They terrorize them." Says Link.

"They are constantly trying to take over the waters away from Ameena's father, King Neptune, who is the God of the waters of the Earth. They want to not only take over the waters but all of the earth as well. They are in league with some surface dwellers of whom we don't know yet." Link continues.

"Between them they want to rule the world. We call them Pencil Heads because their heads look like what you humans call pencils. They sort of look like broken pencils though because their body bends and they have four feet and long thin arms that they can wrap around you and choke the very life out of you. They can even tie them in a knot being so thin. It is hard for them to hold anything in their hands because they're not really hands. They are nubs with only one suction cup that isn't very strong and can hardly hold anything." Link takes a breath and continues;

"They don't actually swim but scurry along the bottom of the ocean and hop. They can hop pretty far in the water as they are hollow inside and kind of float. If their bottoms were not solid and a little heavy they would float away. Cut their bottoms off and they probably would float away. But be careful of their heads. They come to a sharp point and can pierce almost everything in the waters. They also have an eye on the front and back of their head and can see in all directions and they hardly ever sleep."

After this long explanation Link seems to be tired and closes his eyes.

"HEY, WAKE UP!" yells Amphi.

Link gives a violent jump backwards and opens his eyes.

"No need to yell" he says shaking his head sending his hair all around it in a swirl.

"Have a little consideration for an old fellow. I'm 300 years old you know. Oh yeah, you don't know do you. Well now you do. Be a little patient with me . . . . Now where was I?" He asks.

"You were telling me about the Pencil Heads," says Amphi laughingly, "and you fell asleep."

"I wasn't sleeping," says Link defensively. "Just checking if you were listening to me and paying attention."

"Sure," says Amphi again laughing, "that was a good test." he says with a big grin.

"Humph!" grunts Link, "You think your so smart. We'll see when I start teaching you."

"When will that be," says Amphi impatiently.

"How about right now." replies Link. "There are sharks hiding in the seaweeds around here and you are going to practice stunning them."

"SHARKS!! STUNNING SHARKS!! ARE YOU CRAZY OR DO YOU THINK I AM??" Amphi is looking all around for the sharks. Not seeing any, he calms down and says:

"Can I really stun a shark? Are you serious? Do I have that power?" Amphi is amazed at this.

"Is this going to be my first power or my only power?"

He asks Link, with wide eyes.

Link is practically doubled over with laughing so hard at Amphi's amazement and wide eyed look.

"No, it is your third power." he says trying hard to stop laughing.

"Your first power you are already using, it is called telepathy and you have been using it since you became conscience remember?" Link reminds him.

"Oh . . . Yeah, that's right." says Amphi remembering.

"What is my second power?" He asks, puzzled.

"Your breathing and talking! Sheesh." says Link "What did you think it was?" He continues, shaking his head.

"Oh . . . . Yeah of course . . . DUH." Amphi says hitting himself on the side of his head with the flat of his hand.

"We will develop your other powers later on or you may discover them yourself." Link assures him.

"My other powers?" Inquires Amphi.

Ignoring the question, Link says:

"Now, in order to stun something or someone, you have to concentrate hard on a blue beam coming out of your fingers and point at the object or thing you want to stun. A bluish almost invisible beam will shoot out and stun them. Remember concentrate on a blue . . ." ZZZAP! A sizzling sound like something frying, than a bang, and Link is stunned before he could finish talking. It seems Amphi was concentrating while Link was talking and pointed at him.

"Oh oh, now how do I unstun somebody." says Amphi laughing but worried at the same time.

"You look funny standing there with your mouth open like that Link." says Amphi laughing gliding towards Link. He reaches for Link to close his mouth when CURACK! A loud snapping sound and Link regains his senses saying: ". . . beam." Amphi jumps back in surprise tumbling head over heals in the water with eyes as big as saucers.

"WOW!!!" he says. "You scared me half to death just now." He says when he regains his 'footing' on the ocean floor.

"The stun only lasts a few minutes so when you use it you have to move fast to do what you want to do before they come out of the stun." Link explains.

"They don't even know they've been stunned until they notice your not there or something has changed. They don't feel anything when they get stunned." He adds as an after thought.

"I see," says Amphi, laughing out loud.

"So you don't know that I just stunned you?" He asks.

"You did?" says Link.

"I've never been stunned before . . . . I think. I wondered why you were so close to me and why you were doing backward summersaults. Well it's true then . . . They don't feel a thing, because I didn't. Now go practice on the sharks in the seaweeds." He tells Amphi seeming to be a bit disturbed at him for stunning him.

"You have to actually see them to be able to stun them. So you have to lure them to you or go in there and find them before they find you and eat you." He says to Amphi, with a big smile on his face.

Amphi heads for the weeds but hesitates before going in. Still very unsteady on his feet and not too sure of being able to swim amongst the weeds.

"Aren't you coming in with me?" he says to Link.

"No . . . This you have to do on your own." Link replies.

"How will you know if I'm stunning them if your not going in with me?" he asks.

"I'll hear the zaps and the cracks." replies Link.

"What happens if I miss and they get me?" Amphi asks, not really wanting to know the answer.

"Oops . . . no more Amphi." says Link with a wide grin. "After you've stunned at least five sharks then you'll be ready for the Pencil Heads." He adds.

"FIVE SHARKS! I'VE GOT TO STUN FIVE SHARKS? HOW MANY SHARKS ARE IN THERE?" He asks.

"Quite a few and all with razor sharp teeth." answers Link.

Enjoying Amphi's discomfort tremendously.

"Go on now or are you afraid?" Link prods him, smirking.

"I'm not afraid of anything!" replies Amphi, but not very convincingly, looking closely at the wall of seaweed.

What Amphi doesn't know is that the sharks know that they are there for that purpose and wouldn't eat him if he does miss. This was pre-arranged by the Goddess Ameena.

Amphi enters the seaweed bed very cautiously. The weeds are thicker then he realized. It's like walking in a corn field but with no rows separating the stalks. As he brushes aside some seaweed he suddenly comes face to face with a shark. He feels the hair on the back of his neck raise up and the blood drains from his face, making his face seem pure white. He couldn't run or swim if he wanted to. He is rooted to the ocean floor just as solidly as the seaweeds are. The shark seems to be the same way for it just sits there staring at Amphi. I guess because it didn't expect to see a human on the ocean floor. The shark knew that someone or thing was going into the weeds to stun him, but it didn't know who or what it would be. They are both frozen as if time itself is standing still. Then suddenly it attacks and Amphi just as suddenly points, and **ZZZAP!** the shark is stunned.

"WOW," exclaims Amphi out loud and now, discovering that he can move, does so immediately, moving away from the shark. He doesn't know if he messed his pants or not due to being in the water and being soaked anyway. He sure felt like he did. The shark was so big he thought.

"I hardly had to concentrate at all. I just pointed and thought of stunning it and it happened." He says as if explaining it to somebody there with him.

After a few minutes **CURACK!** and he knows the shark is back to himself again. He quickly, if you call moving at a snails pace quickly, struggles with the seaweed to go further in, to find another shark.

"Wait a minute," he says to himself again out loud and stopping his forward motion.

"Why not do this the easy way and stun the same shark four more times?" he asks himself.

He thinks this is a good idea and turns around, only to find the shark or another shark, (who can tell the difference,) heading right for him. He points and **ZZZAP!** that one goes blank. Turning to run or swim whatever, he confronts another one. **ZZZAP!** that one is out too. **CURACK!** Oh-oh here comes the first one he thinks. Ducking down in the weeds he sees the shark or a shark just above him. **ZZZAP!** and **CURACK!** almost in unison as the previous one regains its movements. Stunning them is like paralyzing them so they can't move from that spot 'till the stun wears off. Luckily it's only a few minutes, because, depending on the type of shark, if they stop moving for very long they will drown. It's in the moving through the water that forces the water into their mouths so they can get oxygen and be able to breathe. It's called ram ventilation. Therefore some sharks have to continuously move to stay alive or even sink to the bottom. It's their swimming that keeps them buoyant. That's why if they get caught in a net they die. They have to move even while sleeping, (which they hardly ever do), and then they keep one eye open even while sleeping. They are also cousins to the manta rays and sting rays.

"I've got to get out of here," he thinks, "before they all come at me at once."

Just as he thinks this to himself **CURACK!** He turns to go and two of them are heading for him. Quick as a wink he points at one then the other **ZZZAP!** . . . **ZZZAP!** And he heads out of the weeds, as he nears the edge of the weed bed he hears, **CURACK!** . . . **CURACK!**

Amphi goes casually, gliding on his back, out of the weeds blowing on his fingertips as if he had shot the sharks with them, as indeed he had, so to speak.

"Nothing to it," he exclaims.

"Those sharks were like little puppy dogs. Now where is that Pencil Head castle?" He continues feeling like he's nine feet tall.

Link is looking at him puzzled and says:

"Puppy dogs???"

"Yeah, puppy dogs, you know little furry creatures." Amphi says.

Link is holding his nose and says:

"I don't know what those are or what you did, but you reek and there's brown stuff coming out of the bottom of your pants."

Amphi's eyes go wide as dinner plates and he bolts for the seaweeds again. He is in the weeds for a while and Link is starting to think that the sharks got him when he comes back out of the weeds looking ashamed and all red faced. But he doesn't smell anymore.

"I fell into some kind of muck hole that stunk real bad in the weeds and I guess I got some on me." He tells Link, as an explanation. Link decides not to push the issue.

"You only had to stun five how come you did six?" Link asks Amphi.

"I didn't feel like being fish food." says Amphi trying hard to make light of the situation.

"Just my luck." says Link, so low Amphi doesn't hear him good.

Amphi says, "What? What did you just mutter?" He's still feeling ashamed although he feels that Link doesn't realize what was wrong.

Link laughs. "I said the castle is a long way from here." replies Link. His laughter makes Amphi feel a little better now.

"Oh, okay. But, if it is a castle, and it is on the ocean floor, how come we have to use the gates to get in? Why can't we just swim over the walls?" Amphi inquires.

"Because they have a huge net going from the top of the walls up over the entire castle. The net is made of some kind of material that we have never seen before. You can't cut it . . . . At least we haven't been able to." replies Link.

"Oh. Okay. Do you have sea horses or a car or something to get there with?" Asks Amphi, frowning not sure if Link was serious or not or even if he heard him right when he muttered.

"Sea horses? Cars?" Link laughs loudly, "Haw . . . haw . . . haw where do you think you are, in the city or something? You are so funny sometimes. You make me laugh."

Amphi looks confused and says, "So do we swim or walk?"

"Look at your feet and calves, and you tell me." says Link.

Amphi looks down at his feet and is surprised to see that they are longer and have webbing between his toes which seem to have grown longer also and he has fins on his calves.

"**When did that happen**???" Amphi asks big eyed.

"Look at your hands and your arms." Says Link again looking very amused at Amphi's expressions.

Amphi lifts his arms up and is more surprised to see that his fingers are longer and have webbing between them and there are fins on his forearms up to his elbows like Link. What's more he looks closer at his arms and discovers they have scales on them, fine little ones, but scales nonetheless. They are green and covering his body, makes Amphi green.

"**What the!!!**" he can't finish so surprised is he.

"**Link!!!**" He cries! "**When did this happen?** They weren't like this a minute ago when I came out of the weeds! **What are you doing to me?**" He is trembling now, so fearful is he.

Link is almost doubled up with laughter again as he watches Amphi discovering the changes in his body.

"You should see your head." says Link.

"**What about my head?**" asks Amphi, quickly putting his hand up to his head, and a look of amazement comes over his face as he runs his hand over the top of his head. He feels that it suddenly stretches up and out towards the back and comes to a sharp point about a foot long. His hair, which is closely cut, stops at the base of the point and the point itself feels like a bone that was sharpened with a pencil sharpener. Actually it feels like he has a racing helmet on that he can't take off his head. On further inspection, feeling down the side of his head, he discovers that his ears have fins on them also and they are moving very fast and seem to be vibrating.

"**What is happening to me?**" He asks Link looking as scared as he feels and starting to look around wildly.

"That's the magic of the Goddess Ameena. She has changed you so you're more able to handle yourself here in the deep. She is always aware of what you are doing and where you are." Link explains, again very calmly.

"You are her Prodigy and she will look out for you. But you still have to figure things out for yourself too. She will supply the tools but you have to supply the know how." continues Link.

"Did you also notice that you are no longer fighting the current and are more steady on your feet?"

"Hey! You're right! I do feel more comfortable now. What happened? How come I can do this now?" Amphi asks forgetting that he was annoyed at the changing of his body and thinking that he was becoming a fish.

"That's because of the fins you now have. They are what steadies us in the water, and what makes us able to hover or float any where in the water at whatever depth we want. Your fins on your arms and legs will quiver when you are hovering, keeping you upright, like you are right now. They will do this automatically without you thinking on it. The fins on your ears will keep you in balance, again automatically without you thinking about them. Those along with the dorsal fin on yourback will keep you from rolling and tumbling in the water. Your hands will be your means of steering in whatever direction you want. Your feet, well if you don't know what they will do, then you are in big trouble. You now have the instincts of us water beings and should be able to turn and move just as fast as we do."

This was a long speech for Link and again he looks like he's about to fall asleep.

Amphi shakes his head like he's in a daze and says;

"I'm beginning to understand now. With my family gone, this is my world from now on isn't it? I am still human and think and feel like a human, but have the workings of a fish."

"Yes, you are part of the ocean world now and have a lot of learning to do, to be able to survive in it, as the rest of us do. We are learning all the time. It won't be easy and it will take a while to get used to this new life." Link says sighing.

"I hope you are a fast learner as I kind of like you and it would sadden me to see you get eaten or caught or something . . . . At least I would be saddened for a little while anyway. You will find there are many, many things to watch out for in the ocean. You have to develop your fish instincts a lot more so as not to fall prey to a lot of different dangers that we fish have to be constantly aware of." Link warns him.

"Like what kind of dangers?" Amphi asks.

"Well, like changes in the water temperatures; the sounds or lack of sounds that warn of approaching danger; trolling fish nets; hungry sharks on the prowl; humans spear fishing in scuba gear; and in your case just pleasure divers out for sport and spotting you. You would scare the daylights out of them and possibly make them drown. Deadly and toxic trash that humans discard in the sea. These are just a few dangers, there are many, many more, but we don't have time to really get into them right now." Link tells him.

They both pause for a few minutes digesting this knowledge and it is a very somber moment. For Amphi is just now fully realizing that this is not a game where you can quit at any time, like his fantasizing that he's a buccaneer. His dream of finding a deserted island and pretending to be the Robinson Crusoe family doesn't even come close to what is really happening to him. In all his fantasies, he never envisioned anything as wild as this. This is for real. There is no going back to what he was. Reality can be so cruel and mean he thought to himself. He no longer had a family and now he no longer had any friends either. The surface world was lost to him from now on. He had begun to tear up with all these thoughts so he shook his head and said.

"Okay . . . enough of this! Lets go to the Pencil Head's castle." exclaims Amphi.

"It is about a day and a nights swim from here, in the warmer ocean, so you can practice your new power while we travel," exclaims Link, "now lets go."

"Wait a minute. What do you mean by warmer ocean?" asks Amphi.

Link says. "It's the part of the waters that is warmer than these. We travel southwest and west about a thousand or so miles 'till we pass the land then turn northward a couple hundred miles and we are there."

"Oh, you mean in the Pacific ocean." says Amphi.

"Is that what you call it?" asks Link. "We just say the warmer waters."

"Ok! Lets go then, what are you waiting for." Amphi says teasingly.

Link just shakes his head and heads out kind of south-westward. It doesn't take long for Amphi to see why Link said it was about a day and a night's trip to reach the Pencil Heads castle. Unlike the turtle that he kind of resembles, Link travels quite slow. Remember he is 300 years old too. So after two days of training and traveling, (they slept at night), they arrive at the Pencil Heads castle. Many denizens of the deep were stunned without even realizing it on the way.

It was kind of funny watching an octopus floating in its own ink spray for a few minutes before darting away. A manta ray coming close to see who we were and suddenly we are not there and he swims away, as if flying, with his huge wings flapping. A shark that was about to attack and then there was nothing to attack because we were gone after stunning it. The funniest one was when a barracuda came darting out from its hiding place to attack and got stunned. The puzzled look on its face, when it came to its senses, made both Link and Amphi laugh as it looked all around then slowly backed back into its hiding spot. It must have been thinking, "What did I come out here for?" All the denizens were unaware that they had been stunned and none of them were hurt.

CHAPTER 4

PENCIL HEADS CASTLE

The castle is a huge, dark and foreboding looking ugly thing. It has high towers seemingly all over the place. On all the corners, and there are many corners, along the walls and the ones inside the castle, some standing taller than the ones on the walls. Big dark windows that are high up through which every once in a while you could see a Pencil Head go by them. The whole thing seems to be covered with a mesh so no-one could enter from above. The castle extends for miles under the sea. There are gates to get in and also gates inside to go in further, and still more gates beyond those gates.

"Okay," Link says, "We're at the first gate to get in. You know how to deal with these guys."

"I do? . . . . I mean I do." says Amphi.

"Concentrate on that blue beam and point," whispers Link.

Amphi says to himself "Okay, I know how to do this."

Quickly approaching the Pencil Head guarding the gate he points and ZZZAP! Amphi stuns his first enemy.

Link says hurriedly, "Now go through the gate and stun some more Pencil Heads."

"Yeah! Let's go!!! . . . CHARGE!!!" Yells Amphi. "Yell with me Link . . . . CHARGE!!! LINK? Where did you go? LINK??" Amphi looks around but there's no Link. He disappeared just as suddenly as he appeared.

"Looks like I'm going to have to get the power star by myself," Amphi mutters to himself.

"Here I go." he says out loud going through the gate.

A couple minutes later Amphi finds himself in an ice room in the Pencil Heads castle. It seems he got Zapped himself due to all his foolish yelling.

"That's why Link disappeared," he says to himself under his breath. Out loud he says.

"Now how am I supposed to get out of here?"

"I've been in here for four days. There's only one way out." says a voice from a darkened corner.

"Who said that?" Amphi yells surprised, "Link! Is that you? Show yourself!"

"I did! And I'm not Link." Says a man gliding out of the shadows. He is bigger than Amphi for he is a grown man. He too has gills and fins just like Amphi's, but his head appears normal, except for his ears, which are like Amphi's with fins on them and they are bigger. Bigger, because they have to stick out through his thick long flowing mane of blonde hair. He is tall and kind of handsome and appears very muscular as if he had been a weight lifter when he was on the surface world. Amphi felt sure he must have come from the surface world because he had legs instead of a tail and was wearing jean cut-offs. He too didn't have a shirt on just like Amphi. Come to think of it, I wonder what did happen to my shirt, I had one on, but now it's gone.

"My name is Carbs. I thought I was the only merman who still had his legs and feet. I came here at the bidding of the Goddess Ameena to retrieve the power star for her father. She saved my life when my ship was destroyed by a hurricane. I feel I owe it to the Mer-people for accepting me into their midst after the Goddess

Ameena saved me. She is the most beautiful mermaid I have ever seen and I fell deeply in love with her. She loves me too. If I can bring the power star back for her, then maybe her father will allow us to marry." He explains to Amphi.

"And who might you be," he asks.

"My name is Jam . . . Uh . . . Amphi." Amphi says.

"Well Jam uh Amphi why are you here?" Carbs asks.

"No . . . No my name is just Amphi. It used to be Jamie but it is now Amphi. I have to get used to it that's all." Amphi explains sheepishly and a little embarrassed.

"Well okay then, Amphi, what brings you here?" Carbs asks again.

"I too have come to rescue the power star for the Goddess Ameena but not because we are in love. She saved my life also when our boat exploded and I sank into the ocean and . . . well it's a long story that I'd rather not tell right now, okay?" Amphi responds.

"Okay. So maybe we can work together and get the star. There's only one way out and that's through this little hole in the wall. I'm too big to fit through it. I'm not sure what's on the other side but I hear slapping sounds every so often coming through there." explains Carbs quickly.

"I think I once saw a tentacle, like an octopus' tentacle but it was huge. A lot bigger than I've ever seen on an octopus." He says.

Amphi asks, "Have you tried sticking your arm through there?"

"Are you kidding? After seeing that tentacle you think I'd stick my arm through there? I'm brave but not that brave. I'm not stupid either." replies Carbs.

"Besides, I probably could have put my arm through there when I was first put in here, but it's too thick to reach the other side now. It grows thicker every day." Carbs explains.

"Well I could probably fit through there but if I did how'll that help you get out?" Amphi asks looking around the room for a door or some kind of entranceway.

"I don't see any doors that I could open from the other side to release you," he says.

Carbs says, "That's why I was in the shadows there. I discovered a crack in the wall that could be the edge of a doorway. Come over here and I'll show you."

Amphi goes over to the corner and sees the crack himself but it looks like only a crack not like a doorway. He thinks that it was wishful thinking on Carb's part that he thought it was a doorway. Not wanting to argue with him, Amphi doesn't say what he thinks.

"The wall wasn't as thick four days ago when I first found myself in here and I think the room is getting smaller" Carbs says.

"You mean the walls are getting thicker while we are in here now?" Amphi says with fear edging in his voice.

"Yes, I think that eventually they will close in on us and we'll be caught in a solid block of ice if we don't get out soon." replies Carbs just as fearfully as Amphi. So much so that his voice actually trembles. Amphi notices that Carbs is shuddering and realizes that it wasn't fear that was in his voice but that he is very cold and is shivering.

"It is getting colder in here since I came in." He says to Carbs.

"Do you feel it too?" asks Carbs shaking his arms.

"I think we better get out of here fast before we freeze to death long before the room turns into an ice cube." Amphi exclaims with feeling and shaking his arms too.

"I'm going through that hole and see what I can do to get you out," he states.

"Be careful," Carbs says, "I just know there is some kind of monster out there. You have to be prepared for anything."

"Don't worry," Amphi replies, "I have stunning power that the water Goddess gave me, uh, your girl friend that is. I'll stun anything that moves when I go into the hole and when I get out of the hole as well."

Amphi enters the hole and discovers that it is like a long tunnel. It is growing longer even as he is crawling along the bottom and he knows that the room he just left has to be getting smaller. It will very soon be a block of ice trapping Carbs inside if he can't get him out. This realization makes him go faster and he has to caution himself to slow down and be alert for danger.

As soon as he gets to the end of the tunnel he sees a giant octopus that is sleeping just outside. Thankful that he practiced stunning octopuses on his way over here he quickly concentrates on the blue beam and ZZZAP! the octopus is stunned and Amphi scurries right past it when CURACK! the octopus is again sleeping soundly. It didn't know it had been zapped and that Amphi had gotten out of the tunnel. He starts to look around for a door or something that looks like a way to get back into the ice room. That's when he notices that the octopus is chained to the opposite wall by two tentacles. This lets him know that the octopus is also a prisoner like they are. Amphi concentrates and tries to communicate with the octopus telepathically.

"Hello!!! My name is Amphi . . . . What's your name big guy?" he asks. He evidently does "talk" to the octopus because it opens its eyes wide and looks around wildly.

"What!!! What!!!" The octopus is thrashing about with its free tentacles in confusion.

"Where are you??? Who are you??? . . . . Please don't hurt me any more." It whimpers pleadingly.

"I'm not going to hurt you, I want to help you." replies Amphi quickly while ducking under the thrashing tentacles.

"Stop with the arms already, you almost took my head off just then." Amphi yells.

"Oh . . . Sorry, you scared me and I thought you were going to hurt me again." the octopus says while it lowers its arms.

"I'm not going to hurt you" . . . He assures him, "What is your name? You do have a name don't you?"

"My friends call me Inky." says the Giant octopus.

"Inky?? That's an odd name." comments Amphi, "Why do they call you Inky?" He asks, hoping to calm this giant beast.

"Because I have so much more ink compared to the other octopuses." Inky responds, now completely still.

"Well I'd like to be your friend also if you'll let me." Amphi quickly states.

"Get me loose from these chains and we will be friends for life." Inky says.

"I'll see what I can do, but will you help me in return?" Amphi asks his new friend.

"Yes . . . . I'll help you do anything you want to do if you can free me." Inky says with his eyes open wide.

"Well first, my friend Carbs is trapped in the ice room here and is about to be engulfed in ice if we don't get him out real quick like." Amphi explains.

"Can you help me get him out right now?" He asks.

"I think so . . . You see my ink comes out very hot and if I blow it against the wall it might melt it. But you have to get behind me or it'll fry you little guy." Inky says.

So Amphi quickly gets behind Inky and says, "Okay . . . . Let err rip."

"Rip??" Inky says. "It doesn't rip." Inky says in confusion.

"Okay . . . Let it flow or blow or whatever. Just do your thing." says Amphi resignedly.

"My thing???" says Inky, puzzled.

"Yeah . . . Let go with your ink already . . . . friend." says Amphi realizing that Inky is slow to understand. That's why he got caught I'll bet. Thinks Amphi.

"Oh . . . Okay, here goes." he says.

And instantly a huge, coal black fluid, shoots forward hard against the wall of ice. Amphi feels the heat even though he's behind this giant octopus. It's almost like a blow torch. If he wasn't behind Inky he would have been bar-b-cued, and well done at that. He can't see anything for a little while and finds it hard to breath with the ink all around the place. As the ink clears, he sees the wall is gone and Carbs is laying on the floor in front of them.

"Carbs!!!" He yells rushing over to him. He is barely breathing and Amphi begins beating on his chest. (He saw somebody do this in a movie once.) It wasn't actually CPR but close enough to do the trick. Carbs gasps and starts to cough pushing Amphi away.

"Stop!! You're pounding me to death." he says gasping.

"Oh . . . Sorry . . . . But I thought you were dead already and it scared me." Replies Amphi.

"You thought I was dead??? I thought I was dead too! I got so cold . . . . The ice kept coming in faster around me. I think the room knew somehow that you got out. I couldn't breath then darkness overcame me and the next thing I know you're beating on my chest, like it's a drum or something." Exclaims Carbs.

"You saved my life. I am forever in your debt." he says.

"Oh stop it, I didn't get you out Inky did." Amphi says, although he's glad that Carbs feels that way. Which means he will forever be his friend.

"Inky? Who's Inky? Oh . . . that must be the octopus floating over there." says Carbs. "Is that his name? How did you tame him so quickly? Octopuses are usually shy and don't associate much with others."

"He's a prisoner, just like us. He's chained to the wall and we just have to free him." Amphi states pointedly.

"His hot inky blast is what freed you from the ice." He adds.

"Well, we most certainly do have to free him then." says Carbs amiably.

"Hello Inky and thank you for getting me out of there." He waves to Inky and Inky waves back with two tentacles saying:

"No problem, friend, I was glad to help. Please free me."

"Where is he chained? Show me." Carbs says.

"Over here, follow me." Amphi swims around behind Inky with Carbs following close behind.

"See, the chain is attached to the wall here and around his tentacle there. I don't know how we are going to free him, but we have to because I told him we would." He says pointing at the huge tentacle nearest him.

"And there is another chain holding another tentacle, so he can't move too far at all." Amphi continues.

Just then a Pencil Head appears from out of a door that suddenly appeared in the wall beside them. He is taken as much by surprise as Amphi and Carbs. Amphi points and ZZZAP! he stuns the Pencil Head.

"Quick, grab him." He yells to Carbs.

Carbs grabs the pencil head and Amphi ties his arms in a knot. Then CURACK! the pencil head starts moving. He tries to run but Carbs is holding him pretty good so he can't move.

He tries to extend his arms but they only make a circle in front of him. He tries to put his arms over Carbs' head but Carbs ducks and hit's him hard in the eye that is in the front of his head. Then reaching up he breaks the point off that forms the top of his head and a green slime begins to run down the Pencil Heads face and starts floating around them.

"Oops." says Carbs. "I guess his brains must be leaking out." he says laughing, but afraid to touch the gooey stuff as it floats by in front of him. The Pencil Head shudders and goes very limp in his arms. Carbs drops him and he doesn't move at all.

"Is he dead?" Asks Inky staring at the Pencil Head.

"I guess I killed him." Says Carbs. "I didn't mean to." He says defensively, "But he was struggling so much and . . . ."

"Well he would have killed us, if he could." interrupts Amphi in defense of Carbs, and to make him feel better because he looks like he's about to get sick.

"He was coming to hurt me some more." Says Inky.

"You did the right thing. Now get that key that's hanging around his neck and lets free Inky." Amphi says with authority.

Carbs grabs the key that's on a seaweed chain around the Pencil Heads neck and with a jerk breaks it loose from him and moving around behind the giant octopus he fumbles with the lock that is holding the chain on his tentacle.

"Hold still." he says roughly. "So I can unlock this blasted thing." Amphi knows he's speaking like that to cover up his feelings for what he just did, because Inky didn't move at all.

"Hello and thank you." Inky says very politely, as Carbs unlocks the other chain too.

"How can I help you guys for doing this?" he asks.

"You can help us recover the power star that the Pencil Heads stole from the Mer-People." Carbs tells him.

"Do you know where they keep it Inky?" Amphi asks not really thinking he would know.

"Yes, I heard the Pencil Heads bragging about that a while ago and they said it was in the tallest tower in the castle. It is locked in a glass tube on display in the middle of the room. If you touch it an alarm will sound that can be heard all over the castle." Inky tells them.

"The alarm is ear piercing for someone did try to touch it and it went off. It almost broke my eardrums, it is so loud." says Inky excitedly.

"That was when I tried to get it." states Carbs. "I don't know how they caught me. I was reaching for the power star one minute and the next I was being carried to the ice room."

"I know how." Says Amphi. "I have stunning power and so does someone else evidently, 'cause that's how they caught me too. But who else would have that kind of power? I thought only the Water Goddess could give someone stunning power." Says Amphi wondering out loud.

"Oh no," says Inky, "The sorceress Andrea can give that power to someone also, but for only a little while. They have to keep taking a potion to keep the power. But if they take the potion for too long of a time then they will in turn be stunned and stay that way forever."

"You are a fountain of information, Inky, how do you know this?" asks Amphi.

"The Pencil Heads were laughing about how they had a secret weapon to use against their enemies. I guess they thought

I would never get out of here and they told me all about it. I've been down here for a long time." Inky says sadly.

"The Pencil Heads did a lot of talking in front of me because they think I'm stupid and slow witted. I'm slow at picking up things, but not so slow witted as they think, and I can remember for a long time." He adds.

"They told me to watch out for whoever would come out of that hole because they would be coming to kill me. That's why I was so scared when you spoke to me." He says turning and talking to Amphi.

"That's alright, Inky, you didn't hurt me and now we're friends. Right?" Amphi replies.

"Right!" says Inky.

"You didn't tell me that you knew where the power star was Carbs. How come?" Amphi says looking hard at Carbs.

"You didn't ask me and I would have told you when we started to look for it. I'm not sure where to go from here, but when we got out in the courtyard of the castle I would have known then." Carbs replies.

"I almost had it too. I didn't know about the alarm 'till I touched it. It scared the heck out of me and that's why they were able to get me. Besides I didn't want you to know that I almost had it and failed." He says dejectedly and with his head bowed.

"Well, don't worry, We know about it now and we'll figure out a way to get it, I hope." Amphi says, not too happy though.

"I'm not very smart and kind of slow, but if we get to the tower and to the room where the star is. When the alarm sounds and the Pencil Heads come I can fill the room with my ink and roast some of them while you stun the others." says Inky to Amphi.

"Hey, that sounds like a good plan to me." says Amphi and Carbs quickly agrees.

"Yeah," he says, "That's a better plan than I can think of. I was just going to grab the star and run."

There's more to Inky than anybody knows, thinks Amphi, while having second thoughts about Carbs. He might be big and have a lot of muscle, but not a lot of brain matter in the head he thinks. Out loud he says;

"Wait a minute! If the alarm is so loud that it caused you pain down here then what will it do to us in the room with it?" asks Amphi.

"What did it feel like to you Carbs?" he asks turning to Carbs.

"I really can't remember too much. It was ear piercing and I remember putting my hands over my ears and starting to fall, then I felt them carrying me to the ice room." Carbs replies.

"That's not a lot of help, but you do remember starting to fall, right?" Amphi states.

"Yeah I guess I probably would have passed out if I wasn't zapped first." Carbs responds.

"That means we will have to block our ears with something before we enter the room so we can't hear the alarm and therefore it won't effect us." reasons Amphi.

"Okay then, lets get moving before more Pencil Heads come looking for this one on the floor." says Carbs.

"What should we do with him?" asks Inky.

"Just leave him here." says Carbs looking disgustedly at the thing on the floor still oozing green slime out of its head.

"Lets get a closer look at him or her or it, whatever it is. So we can know what they are like." says Amphi.

"Okay, but I feel freaky handling it . . . . Again." says Carbs shuddering physically.

He turns the Pencil Head over and they discover that just below his or her rear set of feet, there is a juncture that is like a belt around its body, that's where the weight is that keeps it from floating away. If they cut its body right here than it would float away because the rest of its body appears to be hollow. They pull its arms out as far as they'll go and discover that they can only stretch about five feet from its body.

"Okay, we've seen enough. Lets get out of here." Says Amphi.

CHAPTER 5

THE BATTLE

With that they leave through the door the Pencil Head came through and find themselves in a garden of sorts with statues all around. On closer inspection of the statues they discover that they are really people who are petrified. Evidently they were victims of shipwrecks who drowned or people who fell overboard and were taken by the Pencil Heads to decorate their garden. Now Amphi was glad that his family was blown to smithereens rather than drowning so they couldn't be displayed by these demons. The more he learns about these Pencil Heads the more he hates them. This is a good reason to hate them, he tells himself.

"This is why all the denizens of the deep hate the Pencil Heads." whispers Carbs as though reading Amphi's thoughts.

"Goddess Ameena told me about this before I came here so I could be prepared for it, but how do you prepare yourself to seeing this. These are actual people who deserve to be properly buried and honored." Carbs says seriously. Amphi's respect for him jumps up a notch at these words. There were statues of sharks, whales, squid, porpoises and several other species of fish and shell fish and even coral.

"They have no respect for anything." mutters Amphi as they journey through the garden.

"Lets hurry and get out of here," he says hastily. They swim higher and discover that they can see the highest tower right in front of them; although still at a distance.

"Lets swim for it." says Amphi, "But watch out and don't get too close to the other towers and the walkways. The Pencil Heads can't swim but they can propel themselves off the walkways and out of the windows of the towers and spear us with their heads." Warns Amphi.

"They can also hop pretty high so don't swim too low." Adds Inky, as a Pencil Head hopped towards him but was not high enough and fell short.

Looking down they could see a lot of Pencil Heads scurrying all over the floor of the castle as well as in the towers and walkways. They were undoubtedly hurrying to the high tower to protect the power star.

"We are going to have to fight to get the power star. We have to leave and come back with some weapons." says Carbs.

"No we don't." says Inky, "There is a lot of swords and shields in the tower next to the big one there."

"Okay, lets go get them." yells Amphi just as a squid, about the same size as Amphi, comes up to them.

"Let me help you guys." he says.

"Where did you come from?" says Carbs nervously.

"I was hiding in the garden along with the statues. I escaped from them a while ago and they were looking for me when you guys came along. That's why there's so many of them here now. My name is Squirt, and I want to help."

"Okay, Squirt, follow us to get some weapons to fight with." says Amphi, "Glad to have you join us."

"Hello Squirt." says Inky.

"Do you know each other?" asks Amphi as they swim towards the other tower.

"Yeah," says Inky. "Squirt was one of the guys who always makes fun of me because I am so slow at picking up on things."

"Well Inky is the one who came up with a neat plan to get the star." States Amphi.

"Really?? I'm sorry about that, Inky," says Squirt. "I sure won't make fun of you anymore . . . . Not after this. That is if we get out of this."

"We will." Amphi states positively. "I can feel it in my bones that we will succeed."

"That's alright Squirt, maybe now we can be friends." Inky says hopefully.

"You betcha," says Squirt, "And if anyone pokes fun at you again they'll be poking fun at me too."

Just then they reach the tower where the weapons are. The Pencil Heads were so worried about protecting the star they didn't think of the weapons tower. They are all over at the high tower and only one guard was in the weapons tower.

"I'll stun him through the window." Amphi tells Carbs. "When I do rush in and do your thing with his head."

Carbs blinks hard and swallows when Amphi says this but says. "Alright, but only because I have to. I don't like having to do this."

"Remember Carbs, its either them or us. They would kill us in a heart beat if they catch us." He explains.

"This is war between them and us." He adds.

"I know." Says Carbs, "But that doesn't mean I have to like it, does it?"

"No . . . No I don't like it either. But we have no other choice do we? We can't just stun them and let them come back after us again and we have nothing to tie them up with." Amphi says thoughtfully.

"Maybe we should cut their bottoms off and let them float away." Inky suggests.

"Okay, when I stun him one of you grab a sword and cut off his bottom before the stun wears off." Amphi quickly agrees. "We will have to throw him out the window fast so he can't extend his arms and grab one of us. Remember they can crush us with those arms." He reminds them.

They warily approach the tower coming up beside a window. Amphi peeks in and spots the Pencil Head guard looking out of another window on the opposite side of the room. There is a commotion going on and he is watching it. Quickly and quietly they enter the room through the window without the guard being aware of them. ZZZAP! Amphi stuns the guard and Carbs grabs him while Inky, grabbing a sword from off the wall, quickly lops off his heavy bottom. Carbs throws him out the window just as they hear CURACK! and he begins to drift up towards the mesh covering the castle, waving his arms wildly and extending them as far as he could. But he was too far from the building to grab it. His arms only extend just so far. They are glad to see that no green slime is coming out of his bottom. But looking down they see that several Pencil Heads are looking up at them because they heard the crack of the stun wearing off.

"Hey, that was a good idea you had Inky." Says Carbs, happy that he didn't have to kill again.

"I don't like to kill anyone, even if they are bad. Killing isn't nice . . . . even in war." he says. They all nod their heads in agreement with that.

"When we fight the Pencil Heads lets try to just chop off their bottoms." says Amphi, and they all agree.

"Okay, everybody grab a shield and a sword and lets go." he continues anxiously.

"We have to find something to block our ears." Inky reminds them.

"Oh yeah." Exclaims Amphi.

"There's some sponge material here on this table," says Squirt, "but why are we blocking our ears?" he asks.

"So the alarm won't bother us." Replies Amphi.

"What alarm?" asks Squirt.

"You'll find out when we get the star." Says Carbs.

They all break off some pieces of the sponge and stuff them into their ears.

"Can you hear me?" Amphi yells to Carbs.

"What?" Says Carbs. "I can't hear you with this in my ears" he yells back.

Amphi signals them to remove the plugs from their ears and says:

"Wait. I want to try something on you guys, alright?"

"What do you want to try?" says Carbs worried.

"It doesn't hurt to be stunned and you don't even know you were stunned, so I want to see if I can concentrate and stun more than one being at a time," Amphi explains, "by stunning you guys."

They began to squirm and are undecided when ZZZAP! they are all stunned at once. A few minutes later CURACK they are back unaware that they were stunned.

"I don't know if I want to be stunned." says Inky and the others are nodding their heads in agreement.

"Oh . . . . That's okay." says Amphi with a smile thinking what they don't know won't hurt them and he decides not to tell them that he had indeed stunned them already.

"I'll try it on the Pencil Heads when we go to the tower where the star is."

"Good, because I for one didn't want to be stunned." says Carbs, "I was already unconscious once today and don't want to be knocked out again." Amphi only smiles.

"Okay, enough gabbing, lets go to the tower." He says.

Having armed themselves with swords and shields, they now head out of the window and swim towards the tower where the star is. They left just in time for as they go out the window a bunch of Pencil Heads rush into the room. They run to the window and a few of them try to propel themselves at the group of rescuers but fall short and are falling to the floor of the castle.

Some of them tried to stretch their arms out to catch them, and actually, a couple of them did manage to reach Squirts long tentacles trailing behind him, but they weren't able to hold on. The suction power in their one suction cup isn't strong enough to hold their weight, and so they fall to the ground also. The only power they have in their arms is like an anaconda's or boa constrictors squeezing and crushing power, but they have to wrap their arms around the thing they want to crush.

As they approach the tower they see dozens of Pencil Heads on the top of the tower preparing to fling themselves down to pierce the intruders with there heads. Our rescuers are hoping the shields will be strong enough to withstand their assault.

Amphi says, "Parry their attacks, don't let them hit the shields directly or they will penetrate them. Hold the shields at an angle so they bounce off them. They can't stop themselves from falling so if they bounce off they will continue down to the ground."

This proves to be true as they approach and the Pencil Heads dive off the top they are soon on their way to the ground as they do indeed bounce off the shields. Some of them try to grab hold but like with Squirt, they can't hold on to them, and are soon plummeting to the ground with the others. They wait 'till all the Pencil Heads on the top have jumped off then continue on to the windows where more of them are waiting.

"When I stun them Inky, you go in the window and let loose with your hot ink."

"Okay," says Inky.

ZZZAP!, Amphi stuns all the Pencil Heads in the closest window and Inky quickly goes in the window and sprays the room with his ink. As they had hoped would happen, this burns the arms and legs off the Pencil Heads in the room, being as their arms and legs are so thin. There is a lot of bodies just laying around the room when the other three come in through the window. More Pencil Heads come in the room from the door on the other side and they are soon almost surrounded by a lot of Pencil Heads and they prepare to do battle. But there isn't as many now as there were before.

ZZZAP! Inky is stunned, but Amphi sees who did the stunning and he immediately stuns the Pencil Head who did it. ZZZAP! he's stunned and CURACK! Inky is back ready to fight.

"Carbs," yells Amphi, "Grab that Pencil Head and cut off his bottom before he comes to, thank goodness he wasn't aware that he could stun more than one at a time or we'd all be stunned now."

Carbs grabs him and Squirt cuts off his bottom at the same time. As Carbs throws him out the window they hear CURACK! and know that they were just in time. The Pencil Head is floating harmlessly upward towards the mesh covering the castle. As he rises he tries to stun Carbs but misses and ZZZAP! stuns a Pencil Head instead, and Carbs promptly cuts off its hind end. As it rises to the ceiling he hears CURACK! and watches as the Pencil Head waves its arms wildly not knowing what happened to him.

Amphi quickly stuns a group of Pencil Heads and Carbs and Squirt, just as quickly lop off their bottoms, and they are on their way to the ceiling too to join the others. Meanwhile Inky with a sword in each of his eight arms is chopping away very deftly on any Pencil Heads who are within his reach, and that's quite a span, almost from wall to wall. The ceiling is too high for them to worry about the ones floating up there to encircle them with their arms. Soon there are a lot of Pencil Heads floating around up against the ceiling and the mesh as more and more of them are getting their bottoms chopped off and their arms too. It was discovered that chopping their arms off didn't kill them either. (Unknown to our heroes, their arms and bottoms will grow back eventually.)

As the Pencil Heads tried to extend their arms around Squirt, Amphi, Carbs, and Inky they have been cutting them off with the sharp swords. Thank goodness that Inky has eight arms being as big as he is, he makes a huge target. Of course, he's too big for any of the Pencil Heads to get above him so they can't spear him from above and the ceiling is way above Inky's head. Inky is making short work of the Pencil Heads and doesn't seem to care if he's just cutting off their bottoms or where he is cutting them. Remember he has a big score to settle with them. They have been hurting him for a long time and he is getting even with them now. Squirt's arms are longer than Inky's and he has two more than him, so it's not really a problem for him to help protect Inky, being as he's a lot smaller and a harder target than Inky. But it doesn't seem like Inky needs protecting for he's like a demon himself, on a rampage, slashing and cutting all over the place. There is quite a bit of green slime floating all about the room, and not just from Inky's doing. With as many Pencil Heads as there are, it is pretty hard to be accurate with the slashing for anybody. It's not very long until only a few Pencil Heads are left and Amphi signals his friends to put their earplugs in and then he grabs the Power Star.

Immediately a loud piercing siren goes off and everybody is blocking their ears including the Pencil Heads. It seems they can't stand the siren either. They are rolling on the floor in pain.

Amphi had dropped the power star when the siren went off, even with the earplugs the alarm is piercing, and it had skidded across the room. Everyone was so busy blocking their ears that no-one noticed it right away. That didn't last long though and soon there was a mad dash for it. Fortunately Squirt is quicker than everybody else and scoops it up with a long graceful sweep of his tentacle suctioning it tight so no-one could grab it from him. Handing it over to Amphi, the foursome quickly scoot out the window, before the Pencil Heads can attack them again. They are out of there and on their way to where, they don't know. All they care about is getting out of that room and away from the tower.

CHAPTER 6

THE ESCAPES

"How do we get out of here now? They'll have all the gates blocked." asks Amphi puzzled.

"I know a secret passage, follow me." Squirt says as he heads for the garden where they entered. They swim fast as the Pencil Heads are trying to follow them on the ground. They swim over the other buildings in the castle whereas the Pencil Heads have to go around or through them. So they reach the garden long before any Pencil Head shows up. Squirt knocks over a statue of a squid and there is a tunnel under it.

"Quick in the tunnel." yells Squirt, and they all go into the tunnel except Squirt.

"What about you, Squirt." inquires Amphi.

"I have to stay here and stand the statue back up," says Squirt bravely.

"But the Pencil Heads will get you." Amphi exclaims alarmed.

"No they won't, cause I'll pretend to be a statue and mix with the other statues of squid. Then when they leave I'll sneak out through the tunnel and meet you guys later." Squirt explains.

"Where will you meet us and how will you know where we are?" Amphi asks, not believing him.

"Meet me at the old shipwreck. Inky knows where." Squirt says confidently.

"Don't worry I'm no brave hero who's going to give up his life for anybody. I know how to do this . . . . Trust me." Squirt assures him.

"Okay . . . The old shipwreck then . . . . See you there soon." replies Amphi, and he joins the others further in the tunnel.

They can't hardly see anything because the tunnel is dark.

"We need Squirt's cousin Lumina or Shiny here," whispers Inky.

"Where is Squirt?" He asks louder looking back beyond Amphi.

"He had to stay to stand the statue back up while we escape." says Amphi.

"He'll be coming soon to meet us at the old shipwreck, Inky. He said you would know where that is." He said this quickly as Inky was starting to go back along the tunnel.

Inky stops and turning around he says.

"Yeah . . . I know where that is. That's where the gang hangs out that always teases me."

"Well they won't tease you as long as you're with us." says Carbs, "Right guys?"

"Yeah!" They both say in unison and it echoes along the tunnel like a lot of 'yeahs'.

"Okay . . . lets go then and get out of here. I don't know where we will come out at." Amphi says, worried.

"I think it won't be far from the old shipwreck." replies Inky.

Inky no sooner finishes talking when they find themselves at the old shipwreck and the Water Goddess Ameena is waiting there for them.

"How did we get here so fast?" Inky asks astonished.

"I brought you here." says the Goddess Ameena.

Amphi stops and stares in wonderment. Before him floats the most beautiful creature he has ever seen. She is hovering just a foot off the bottom and she is exactly what he had always imagined a mermaid to look like. She didn't have any feet but a tail instead. The rest of her was as a human woman with long, thick, flowing golden hair that encircled her like a robe. Her features were delicate but strong and her eyes the bluest he'd ever seen. She had a nose and mouth but still had a set of gills just under her jawbone. This suggested to Amphi that she too could breath out of the water as he could. She had white, white skin and long slender fingers with webbing between them as he had. But her hands were smooth and unwrinkled and looked soft and dainty. In her right hand she held a wand with a star on the end of it and she looked like a royal princess, which of course she was. I guess she was anyway being the daughter of a king, who was also a God, and that made her a Goddess. So she was both a Princess and a Goddess.

"You did very well." The Goddess Ameena says to Amphi.

"This is the reason I saved you and gave you the stun power. I neglected to give Carbs any powers before he left to get the star. I wanted him to stay as natural as possible and hoped that would be good enough. I didn't count on the sorceress Andrea to interfere. It was she who designed the ice room and gave the Pencil Head the stun power. I knew Carbs was locked in the ice room, but I have no powers in the Pencil Heads castle. I knew the only way out was through a narrow tunnel so I needed a boy such as you to help him."

"How did you know I was going to need to be saved?" Amphi asks.

"I didn't. Before your boat blew up I was searching all over the oceans for any one small enough to crawl through the hole in the wall of the ice room." She replied.

"If someone else as small as you was in need of help I would have taken them, but you came along and so I chose you. And, I might add, I'm glad I did for you did an excellent job of not only saving my boy friend but in saving Inky and helping Squirt too."

Amphi looked surprised.

"Oh yes, I know about Inky and Squirt and what they did also. I can see what is going on, but cannot interfere in the Pencil Heads castle. Don't worry about the Pencil Heads as their arms and bottoms will grow back in time and they will survive. They are like earthworms and lizards, their parts will grow back. That was a brilliant idea you had Inky of chopping off their bottoms instead of their heads."

Inky squirms uncomfortably and murmurs, "Thank you, your highness," and quickly turns red all over as octopuses can change color to match their environment, all though, that's not why he turned red just now.

"Why did Link leave me there alone like that?" asks Amphi pouting.

"I told him not to enter the castle for he would hold you back. I knew you would get captured and I counted on that for you to get in the ice room with Carbs. Link would be too slow and awkward for you to have to worry about." Goddess Ameena tells him.

"I understand now, but it was very confusing then and it scared me. I wish you or he had told me that I would be alone." says Amphi still pouting.

"Well, this way you didn't have time to worry about being alone and therefore you acted instinctively as I knew you would." Replies the Goddess Ameena.

"Ah . . . Squirt will be here shortly to join you. I see he has already left the Pencil Heads castle, but he had to do something else first before leaving there. They never knew he was there under their noses. He has done that before and gotten several things for me out of their castle. But he couldn't get to the power star. That was too dangerous for him to do alone. He has been a big help to my father and myself for many years."

"He has?" asks Inky in surprise, still red and now getting a deeper red, from daring to speak to the water Goddess.

"I always thought he was a little wise guy who always played tricks on me." He finishes.

"That's part of his still being a youngster." Goddess Ameena says. "I told him to continue acting as a youngster for a cover for what he was doing for my father and me. This time he got captured though, and they were going to put him to death and mount him in their garden of infamy, if he didn't manage to escape."

"They still don't know how he gets in and out of their castle. He just helped another to escape with him." she continues explaining.

"Huh . . . What did you say? He helped someone else just now?" Amphi asks in amazement.

"Yes, remember the commotion that distracted the guard in the tower?" she asks.

They all nod their heads, remembering.

"Well it was a little girl who fell overboard from a yacht and the Pencil Heads were going to make a statue of her even though she was still alive. Squirt got her away and is bringing her here. I have given her gills so she can still breath and put her under a spell. When Squirt gets here I wish you will help him return her to the surface. She is unconscious under my spell and won't remember a thing when you return her to her people." Goddess Ameena continues.

"You can leave her on a small island that I will raise up out of the deep. Her family will stumble upon this island, which I will place directly in their path, once they discover that she's missing. They are headed north now and when they discover her missing they will turn back south. They will think that they passed the island during the night while they were partying." Explains Goddess Ameena and continues:

"They still don't know yet that she has fallen overboard for they are partying and having a good time on the boat. They evidently think that she is still in her bed sleeping. Which she was, until she woke up, due to all the racket they were making. She fell overboard when she tried to go out to see her mother. The Pencil Heads scooped her up right away before I had a chance to reach her. For some reason my magic was interfered with and I think it was the work of the sorceress Andrea. When you have left her on the shore of the island I will remove the gills from her neck."

"I wish I could have saved your family too, Amphi, but there was nothing left for me to save except for you." The Goddess Ameena says very sadly.

This brings tears to Amphi's eyes and the Goddess Ameena quickly goes to him and hugs him tightly.

"We will be your family from now on and we love you." she says lovingly.

"Yeah . . . . We all love you," says Inky and Carbs again in unison.

"You all right now?" she asks him, loosening her hug on him, and letting him catch his breath.

Rubbing his eyes, Amphi says, "Yeah, I'm alright I just . . . . Well I can't forget what happened that's all. I love you guys too!"

"Well let me have the power star and Carbs and I will go give it to my father. You know why we are giving it to him together don't you Amphi." Goddess Ameena says to Amphi, releasing him.

"Yeah . . . I know why, so you two can get married right?" says Amphi handing her the star.

"Right!" says Carbs and Goddess Ameena together.

"We both love you for what you have done for us and will never forget this. I hope you come to see us often, when we settle in my fathers castle. We, my father and I, will have a lot more things for you to do if you are willing." The Goddess Ameena says as they swim away arm in arm.

Just then Squirt appears around the hull of the old shipwreck.

"Hi fellas," he yells as he comes near. "I told you I'd be okay." He was carrying the little girl in his arms like a baby. She looked like a little doll and they would think that she was one if they didn't see her breathing and the Goddess Ameena hadn't told them who she was. She looked like she was sleeping and that made them whisper.

"We heard what you did and what you have been doing from the Goddess Ameena. I thought you said you were no hero?" Amphi whispers in fun.

"You can talk louder." says Squirt. "She is under a sleeping spell that the Goddess Ameena put on her 'till we can get her on land."

"Well then, HAIL THE CONQUERING HERO!!" He yells.

"HIP-HIP HOORAY!!!!" they both yell and they join arms and tentacles around Squirt.

"Okay! Okay!" Yells Squirt, "But we have to get this child to safety before we can celebrate."

"Goddess Ameena said that the boat is headed north and will turn around when they discover her missing so we must hurry and find the boat to know just where they are headed." He continues.

"The Goddess Ameena will guide us to the island once we locate the boat."

With this they quickly set out with their little bundle of joy, at least they think she is a little bundle of joy to her parents, to locate the boat. They feel that her parents would hurt real bad if they discovered her missing. Being nighttime on the surface gave them time to catch up to them before they became aware she was missing. Of course, if they thought of checking on her before retiring themselves then they would know she was missing. Amphi was hoping they were too busy partying to do that.

Amphi says, "Let me go to the surface and see where the boat is. Wait here while I look."

With that he quickly swims upwards and looks around when he reaches the surface. He can't see the boat so he returns and tells them that he will swim on the surface while they follow him just under the surface.

"That sounds like a good plan." says Squirt.

"But Inky, you carry her, my arms are getting tired and I've been switching them off every once in awhile. She might be little but she gets heavy after awhile."

Amphi suspects that this wasn't really the reason he was giving her to Inky. In the water the little girl didn't weigh much at all. Inky is like a big kid himself and Squirt noticed him looking lovingly at the little girl, so he was letting him carry her and it made Inky feel like he was part of the group too.

"Sure." says Inky, "No problem, buddy. Give her here." He takes her, ever so gently, from Squirt and cuddles her in his immense arms carefully, as if he thinks she'll break or something. Inky is happy to be included with these great guys. At least he thinks they are great and so does the Goddess Ameena evidently.

Amphi returns to the surface and the others follow him. Amphi swims real fast in a zigzag pattern to find the boat, and the others have to strain to keep up to him. Swimming fast like this makes it look like a shark is swimming due to the point on his head looking like a sharks fin cutting the water. It is getting lighter out and he knows the dawn is breaking, so they may have discovered her missing already. He quickly catches up to the boat and sees that it is indeed headed south letting him know that they have already discovered the child missing. He quickly passes it and soon he sees the island ahead. He dives under the surface and stops his friends. Squirt is nearly breathless.

"You have to slow down a bit." says Squirt gasping, "I haven't 'swum' this fast since I was in grammar school learning how not to get hooked on lures, and how to avoid nets."

"I have never 'swam' this fast before." states Inky. "I thought it was fun." he states not hardly breathing heavy at all. (Remember, both Inky and Squirt 'swim' by means of propulsion of water through funnel-siphons on the back part of their bodies.) Inky can shoot water out about as hard and fast as he can shoot his ink, so 'swimming' fast wasn't really a big problem to him. However, Squirt is a different story. He doesn't shoot water as fast as Inky and therefore had a harder time keeping up to them. That's why he was gasping.

Amphi says. "Okay we're here now, the island is just ahead. Give me the girl and I will take her on shore. You guys can't breathe out of water, I can." With that he gently takes the child out of the grasp of Inky who was unwilling, it seemed like anyway, to give her up.

"Don't worry, Inky, I'm not going to hurt her. I'm just going to lay her on the beach so her parents can find her."

Amphi assures him. His heart is as big as he is, thinks Amphi. "But she's so tiny." he says blubbering.

"Don't worry we'll wait around and make sure they find her. Alright?" Amphi states matter of factly.

"Okay. But be careful and be gentle." Inky says brightly with a big smile on his face.

With that Amphi quickly swims to the shore and they watch from out on the ocean as he emerges, walking upright like a human, and gently lays the little girl on the sandy beach. Looking back at his footprints he notices that they look like someone who was walking with flippers on their feet. He is amazed at the fact that he can now breath through his nose. He very quickly takes some deep breaths enjoying the feeling of the air going through his lungs. Breathing the water through his mouth and out his gills doesn't feel that way. After brushing his footprints off the sand and making sure there was no sign of anyone coming near her, he quickly takes a few more breaths and returns to his friends in the water, and none too soon either, for the boat is just coming into sight. Amphi is again breathing through his mouth and gills.

"Quick, we've got to back off a bit so we don't scare them and stop them from landing here." Squirt says.

Amphi and Inky agree so they go further back in the water and looking back Amphi sees the gills on the little girls neck gradually disappear and finally fade away, like they where never there to begin with. He also sees her start to move her arms and knows she will be alright. He notices that there is a lot of commotion on the boat. They evidently discovered her laying on the beach and were pointing at her on the shore. The little girl had stood up and was waving her arms at them. He goes under the water just as the boat nears the beach. About a half mile off shore he rises to see the people getting off the boat and running towards the little girl and she is running towards them and this makes him very happy knowing that at least this family is still together.

CHAPTER 7

NEW FRIENDS

Upon returning to the old shipwreck. The three of them party and whoop it up along with several other denizens of the deep. They don't tell the others why they are partying . . . . just that they are happy and introducing their new friend Amphi. Amphi meets some of Squirts cousins such as Lumina, who can actually glow in the dark and shine his light like a beacon and his twin Shiny, together they could light up practically the whole shipwreck. Now Amphi understands why Inky had said back in the tunnel that we needed Squirts cousins there.

He meets Tiny, Squirts giant cousin, who just about makes Inky look small. He also meets Bucky and his sister Becky the dolphin duo, who you never see apart from one another or not too far away from each other anyway.

Not the least of his new friends are a couple of crabs who seem to get around quite a bit on the land as well as in the sea. And they have a lot of knowledge about what is happening. It turns out that they are the gatherers of information for the Goddess and her father King Neptune.

There are some sharks and tunas who are quite friendly and willing to help out as much as they can with anything that is happening. Some whitefish and red snappers are also present to join in on the festivities. There are so many new faces and species of fish and other denizens of the deep that Amphi is hard pressed to remember all of them.

There is even some turtles that Amphi is introduced to that he suspects are related to Link. They don't look like Link, but are similar in that they too have extra fins on their legs.

Amphi feels that these cousins of Squirt and Inky along with the dolphins and several others that he has met here tonight would some day come in handy. But in the meantime the three of them agree that the less anybody knew about what they were doing the safer it would be for all of them. After promising not to talk to anyone about their adventures from now on, they continue partying.

It is here that Amphi gets his first taste of seaweed. There is all different kinds and each one has a distinct flavor and color of its own that surprisingly Amphi likes. He has never eaten seaweed before and now he was eating it with relish for he evidently had worked up an appetite with all the things he had been doing.

There was brown ones, that sort of taste like chocolate; black ones, that taste like licorice; white ones, that were like vanilla cream; green, that taste like asparagus and he shied away from them. The gold ones taste like hamburgers and french fries, which is his favorite along with the orange, which tastes like apple pie. A strange looking multi-colored one was juicier than the rest and he felt like he was drinking it rather than eating it. It taste like fruit punch. Needless to say he loves the gold and orange ones more then the rest and pigs out on them along with the multi-colored ones.

As he passes by a doorway in this old ship he spots a mirror on the far wall. Entering the room he goes quickly to it. This is the first chance he has to see himself and he is eager to see what he has come to look like.

He is slightly taken aback when he sees himself. He can see the large fin on the top of his head and he also notices the tiny fins on his ears which had closed up to little pin holes. On looking closer at his face he notices he has fine scales all over it and his nose is also closed up like a skin has formed across his nostrils. His eyes are slightly slanted and they seem to have a film over them, even though he can see clear as a bell. He notices also that even though he has been looking in the mirror for a while, he hasn't blinked even once. He tries to blink, but all that happens is the film over his eyes seemed to move ever so slightly.

Stepping back from the mirror, he examines the rest of his body. twisting and turning to see all around himself. Lifting his legs so to see the fins on his calves. Moving them with his will and being amazed as to how easy it is to make them move the way he wants them to. Doing this makes him glide back towards the mirror and he starts a closer inspection of his face. He notices again how there seems to be a layer of skin closing his nostrils and wonders how it was possible for him to breath earlier in the day when he was on the beach. Now though it would be impossible for him to breath through his nose if he wanted to.

"Of course," he said, "I'm breathing through my mouth now, so I don't need a nose."

Not realizing he said this out loud. He was surprised to hear Squirt say, "No. You don't need a nose. None of us do. Welcome to our world, Amphi."

He hadn't noticed that all had gone quiet and all his friends had slowly gathered in the room behind him. So intent had he been in examining his reflection in the mirror. He also hadn't noticed that Link had joined them.

"I told them all how you came to being down here and what you have done for the Goddess Ameena and the mer-people." Link said.

Amphi looked around at all the new friends he had just made and they all were nodding their heads in approval.

"WELCOME HOME!!!" They all say in unison.

"We are happy that you are one of us and we will show you everything you need to know." Becky states, and all the heads are bobbing.

"Thanks, you guys, I guess I am really one of you now and I know I'm going to need help. But the party isn't over yet is it?" Amphi quizzes not wanting to dwell on himself.

"Heck no," says Squirt. "Lets go back to partying."

With that they all start leaving the room. With a last look in the mirror, Amphi joins them and the party continues 'till everyone starts yawning and gradually find places to bed down. The only ones left awake are Amphi, Squirt, Inky, and Link. Link tells Amphi that he will be teaching him some more, real soon, and that he would gain at least one more new power. Amphi tries his best to find out more about this, but Link won't say anything more except, it isn't time yet. They talk about the happenings that they just went through and decide that they were going to go on more missions together for King Neptune and the Goddess Ameena. With that decision made they call it a night and find themselves places to bed down. Link bids them good night and leaves.

They go to sleep wondering who is the sorceress Andrea?

How is she able to grant powers? And what kind of powers can she give out? These questions haunt them and they are determined to find out more of what is going on down here in the deep. The main question that bothers Amphi the most is:

Who or what were the Pencil Heads? Where did they come from? Why didn't any land dwellers ever catch any of them? Surely some fisherman somewhere should have caught some of them either on their lines or in their nets. They sure weren't like anything he had ever seen or heard of as denizens of the sea. Of course he didn't know what all the denizens looked like and there sure are some strange ones way, way down in the deep. But these guys weren't way, way down in the deep they were right up here amongst us ordinary creatures. He and his friends wanting some answers slept fitfully hoping to go on future missions for the water Goddess and her father King Neptune real soon. Little did they know just how soon that would be.

CHAPTER 8

KIDNAPPED

"AMPHI!! SQUIRT!! INKY!! Wake-up." yells Link excitedly and very loud.

"The Goddess Ameena has been kidnapped!!!" He yells.

"Huh??? What???" Amphi says groggily, "What did you say?"

"THE GODDESS AMEENA HAS BEEN KIDNAPPED!" Link repeats again very loud.

"How can that be??" questions Amphi still in a daze from sleep.

"She's a Goddess and has all kinds of powers." he states still not quite grasping the situation fully.

"How did this happen and when?" asks Squirt.

"Some time last night when everyone was sleeping." says Link woefully.

"What makes you think she was kidnapped?" Amphi asks still not believing it to be true.

"She sleeps in a giant oyster shell and it was overturned and practically destroyed." States Link.

"Somehow they overpowered her and took her away I guess to their castle." He adds.

"The sorceress Andrea had to have put a spell on her." says Inky. "I'll bet that's what happened."

"King Neptune is furious and is ready to empty the ocean to find her if we can't get her back." Link tells them.

"He is gathering an army of stingrays, manta rays, sharks and dolphins to attack the castle. He's gathering everything that swims or crawls to join his growing army. He has told the whales to be ready to bull doze the whole castle the minute they get her out." Link says excitedly.

"We have to try to rescue her before he gathers everybody to do this." States Squirt.

"Isn't that what King Neptune is going to do?" inquires Amnphi rubbing his eyes.

"Why not lets just go with him?" Suggests Inky.

"Do you realize what kind of tidal wave that would cause if he was to bulldoze all that under sea earth?" Link points out.

"It would wipe out all the coast lines along the borders of North and South America and even in Europe." Inky states.

"Not to mention It'll probably swamp the British Isles and Australia." Squirt chimes in.

"It could change the whole face of the earth and destroy a lot of innocent people and sea creatures too." Concludes Amphi.

"This is really serious." Amphi says, now fully awake and beginning to see the picture.

"We have to rescue the Water Goddess as quick as we can." He quickly adds.

"Link, you said I would be given another power. Did I get it yet or is it too late now that the Goddess Ameena has been taken?" Amphi asks.

"You already have the power. You're just not aware of it yet." Link replies.

"Well make me aware of it then and let's get on with the rescue. What is it and how do I use it?" Amphi is all excited at knowing that he already has the gift.

"Okay," Link says "You have the power to make things move just by thinking on it. It's called telekinesis. You have to concentrate very hard."

"Okay." says Amphi let me try it.

He looks at a chair and by the narrowing of his eyes they can see he is concentrating hard. But the chair doesn't move. He shakes his head and tries again. But again the chair doesn't move.

Shaking his head he asks, "Are you sure I've got this power Link."

"Yes you do, it just takes a lot of practice." replies Link.

"We don't have time for a lot of practice though." Amphi says in disgust.

"What good is the power if I can't use it?" he says.

Just then he says, "Shh . . . Everybody quiet. I can hear the Goddess Ameena in my head but it is very faint."

Everybody quiets down, and Amphi strains to hear her.

"Amphi," she says, "Use your powers to get me out of here, I will guide you with my mind when you get close. The Sorceress Andrea, who is my evil cousin, has cast a spell on me and I can't move. I have no power here in their castle. You must hurry as they are planning something big."

Amphi repeats what the Goddess had said and everybody starts talking at once as to what they should do. They were talking so loudly that no-one could hear Link trying to say something. A big bell was hanging from the ceiling and Amphi looked at it and willed it to ring and suddenly it stated to ring real loud. This shut everybody up. They wondered how the bell had been rung when no-one was near it.

Link knew right away and says, "I knew you could do it. You always come through in a pinch. Now make that chair move."

Amphi looks at the chair and whoosh it goes flying across the room. He looks at an old map table that they had used for setting out the seaweed last night and it comes skidding across the floor and stops just in front of Amphi. He looks at Squirt and suddenly he is suspended upside down from the ceiling.

"Hey!" He yells, "What did I do to you?"

"Sorry Squirt. You didn't do anything. I just wanted to see if I could move a live object and you were the closest one and I just knew you wouldn't mind being my guinea pig." Amphi says laughing along with everyone else at Squirts struggling on the ceiling.

"Well put me down before I throw up all over all of you." Squirt responds, starting to gag and act like he's about to throw up and he is immediately on the floor again.

'Wow! This is easy, easier than I thought it would be. I just wasn't sure if I could do it before. I guess I had too many doubts and that's why I couldn't move anything." Amphi suspects.

"Link, why didn't you tell me that the Sorceress Andrea was Goddess Ameena's cousin?" He asks, turning towards him.

"I figured if the Goddess Ameena wanted you to know that, then she would tell you. It's not something she's proud of, you know. Besides how would you like it if someone told somebody something bad about you that you weren't proud of?" replies Link.

"Your right I wouldn't like it, but now I know, so tell me how it came about, that Goddess Ameena can be so good and kind and her cousin can be so evil." Amphi says.

"Well it goes way back when Andrea's father tried to take over all the waters away from King Neptune. There was a huge battle and I don't remember all the details of it. Of course I wasn't there when it happened. It was a little before my time. I'm old, but not that old. My great, great, great grandfather passed the story down through the generations till a lot of the facts got distorted and either got added to or subtracted from the real happening. It was the time when the waters covered the whole world. There wasn't any land at all. But anyway, the gist of it was that Andrea's father was defeated and he never got over the defeat. He killed himself in a fit of rage, cursing King Neptune, after making his daughter promise never to obey him and conferred all his remaining powers over to her. His powers had been greatly reduced during the battle with King Neptune so she isn't as powerful as him but slightly a bit more powerful than the Goddess Ameena." Link tells them, as they stand and stare in amazement at this long narrative from Link.

"But, can she take my powers away that Goddess Ameena gave me?" Asks Amphi.

"No! Only the one who gives the powers can take them away." Link says, but adds "I think anyway."

"You think?? You only think? What will happen if you are wrong and she takes my powers away when we are fighting the Pencil Heads? What happens then? Huh?" Amphi is all excited and worried and doesn't realize that he raised his voice.

"Hey! Calm down Amphi!" Squirt says. "You are in contact with Goddess Ameena. Ask her."

"Oh. You're right Squirt. Let me try to talk with her if I can." Amphi says and closes his eyes in concentration.

He evidently does talk with her as they see a smile slowly coming across his face.

"Okay. I'm sorry Link. You are right, only the one who gives the power can take it away. Unless they perform a ritual which is long and drawn out." The Goddess Ameena told me.

"And in the middle of battle there is no time for any rituals." he adds.

"Now what's the plan for rescuing Goddess Ameena?" Inky asks, joining in with the group.

"Well lets head for the castle and we can all think of a plan on the way." says Amphi.

"But first, Squirt, can you get your cousins to go with us?" He asks Squirt turning towards him.

"Heck, I can get everybody that was at the party last night to go with us." He says.

"Well that's good." says Amphi, "But everybody can't go through the tunnel at once. Most of them will have to wait outside the first gate and after we go in through the tunnel, we'll open the gate for them to come in."

"We'll need Lumina or Shiny to light the way through the tunnel. It is dark in there and with several of us going through we don't want to trip over each other and make a lot of noise."

"Lumina can enter right behind me and Shiny can bring up the rear so there will be enough light for everyone to be able to see." Explains Amphi. "I'll go first so I can stun anybody who sees us. We still have the swords we used the last time so we will take them with us and if I have to stun anyone then we chop their bottoms off and let them float away."

Link looks thoughtful and says, "That may not be the best thing to do."

They all turn and look at him and almost as one voice they say, "WHY??"

Amphi quickly says, "It worked good the last time we did that."

"Well." says Link, in his slow and quiet way.

"You are trying to sneak in there and then open the gate for the others to go in. Right?"

"Right." says Amphi and right away it hits him.

"Oh yeah! If we chop off their bottoms and they float upwards the other Pencil Heads will see them and know that we were in the castle. Why didn't I think of that." he says.

"That's why we are all here now so we can all think together. What one person or being doesn't think of the others will. We are in this together as a team. Right!" Link says.

"RIGHT!" They all say in unison.

"Now what are we going to do with them?" Asks Squirt.

"Why don't we pull their arms out as far as they will go and tie them up with their own arms?" suggests Inky.

"We can tie their feet together with their arms. Can't we?" he asks.

Everybody looks at Inky and there is silence. Suddenly they all yell.

"HOORAY for Inky!!!"

"That's an excellent idea! We don't even have to chop of their bottoms to do that. That way they can just lay there until somebody finds them." Amphi says.

"Link, are you coming with us?" Squirt asks.

"No. I'd like to. But I'll be more in the way, being so slow, and I might get you all caught." Link replies.

"What will you do then?" asks Amphi.

"I'll stay around here and try to keep King Neptune from moving too fast. That way you will have a chance to rescue the Goddess Ameena before he gets there." He answers.

"I don't think we can stop him from smashing the Pencil Heads, but maybe I can keep him from bull dozing them and causing a tidal wave. If we get the Goddess Ameena out he may be happy with just smashing them." He adds.

"Okay then. Lets round up the others and get going." Amphi says.

"Lets all meet right here at the shipwreck and when everybody's here we'll go to the tunnel." He tells them.

With that said everybody splits up and starts to round every one up. It isn't very long before Bucky and Becky join the group. Then comes Tiny along with several other giants like him that weren't there last night but are here now. Along comes Lumina and Shiny and some more of their friends. Soon some friends of Bucky and Becky show up. And not to be excluded from the group a gang of sharks show up and say they want to help too. A couple of large Tuna show up saying that they owe the Goddess Ameena a lot and want to help save her also.

A dozen or so crabs and lobsters show up saying that they didn't know how much help they could be, but they loved the Goddess Ameena also, and wanted to help save her. Maybe they could sneak in without being seen and report back as to what they saw. Squirt reminded them, or told them, that there were a lot of crabs and lobsters in their garden of infamy as statues. This kind of made them back up a little, but they remained firm in that they wanted to help. He then reminded everybody that there were statues of almost every creature in the ocean in their garden so they should be prepared and not be shocked by what they saw. Of course, as it was stated earlier, ocean denizens aren't really close to each other so the main reason for them backing off a little was the idea of them becoming statues if caught.

"Ok then. Tag along with us and try to keep up, and we'll see what we all can do together." Amphi states.

"Squirt, you're the only one who knows where the tunnel is from here. So you'll have to lead the way." Amphi says.

"Okay! Let's get going then." he says and starts off towards the tunnel. As they head to the tunnel Amphi explains to the others that only a few of them will go through the tunnel and the rest will have to wait 'till they opened the gate to be able to enter the castle. He picks the original crew to go in the tunnel. That is Squirt, Inky, and himself along with Lumina and Shiny to light the way.

"Tiny do you know where the first gate is?" He asks turning towards the big guy.

"Yeah, I've been over there with Squirt once or twice." He says, kind of proudly. As if to say look at me, I'm brave.

Smiling a little Amphi says:

"Okay, Tiny will lead all of you to the first gate and be ready to enter as soon as we open the gate, and be ready for anything." He warns.

"The Pencil Heads will be expecting us to try to save the Goddess so they will be prepared and ready." He continues.

CHAPTER 9

THE RESCUE

They reach the entrance of the tunnel and the five of them enter while the others head for the first gate. When they come out of the tunnel and approach the gate from the inside, they know that they were prepared 'cause the guard has a shield to hide behind so Amphi can't stun him. But he's expecting Amphi to come from the front and therefore he is open to Amphi from the rear. Fortunately he is holding the shield behind his back and therefore blocking his vision behind him. Quickly Amphi stuns him, but the stun wears right off real fast, like ZZAP! . . . .

CURACK! That fast. Amphi tries to stun him again and all of a sudden . . . . He can't.

"Oh . . . Oh!!" Says Amphi. He's glad the guard doesn't know he had been stunned. Backing off and hiding behind some seaweed, he quickly concentrates hard to be able to talk to the Goddess Ameena.

"Goddess! . . . Goddess!" He says "We are here in the castle and my stun power isn't working!"

"The sorceress Andrea most have performed the ritual while you where on your way to the castle. You must have left some hair or something of yourself when you were here last." The Goddess Ameena reasons.

"She knows you have it from the first time you were here. I'm glad that I gave you the power of telekinesis so you can still surprise them with that." The Goddess Ameena replies.

"I am being held in the same tower that you got your weapons from the last time you where here but on the floor below. They don't think you'll look for me here. I am tied up lying in what appears to be a human's coffin. There are two guards here waiting for anyone to enter. There is one standing in the open to lure someone into the room and one hiding down behind a half wall at the end of the room. Be careful." She says.

"My cousin, Andrea, may be lurking around here somewhere also, so be extra, extra careful." She warns Amphi.

"Her powers are also useless inside the castle too, but she can still sound an alarm." She advises him.

"I'll keep my eyes open for her and we will be there shortly." Amphi tells her.

With that he goes out and SPLAT he throws the Pencil Head hard against the side of the gate with such force that it knocks him out completely. Squirt ties his arms around his legs and gets the key to open the gate. Unfortunately, when Amphi threw the guard against the gate, he hit the alarm with his shield when it went flying from his grasp. (Remember, they can't hold anything real tight, for they have no fingers just a single suction cup that isn't very powerful.)

There is a loud wailing going on that is alerting the other Pencil Heads that something is wrong. They will soon be coming to investigate.

"Quick unlock the gate!" Amphi yells to Squirt. He really didn't have to tell Squirt that for he was already grabbing the lock to open it. But being excited and nervous he said it anyway and Squirt felt like he wasn't moving fast enough and yelled back:

"I'm going as fast as I can, I've only got ten arms you know."

Amphi says, "Alright . . . Alright I'm sorry. I'm just nervous that's all. Goddess Ameena says they are planning something big and we have to hurry."

"Okay its open . . . Come on in guys . . . Let's hurry 'cause I can hear them coming." He yells out the open gate.

In they all come rushing towards the tower to get more weapons and shields. They very quickly swim higher once they are inside the gate so the Pencil Heads can't reach them. Those who do have shields stay on the lower side to protect the ones without shields. Especially those that don't have a means to hold a shield like the dolphins and the sharks. But they are very quick and can duck anything coming at them. They are also very good with their tails and can hit anything that comes close to them. Any Pencil Heads trying to spear them had better be accurate, because they are so good at batting with their tails, they can send them flying right back into the other Pencil Heads and they end up spearing themselves.

The Pencil Heads are gathering in the tower that holds their weapons and they can see them collecting at the windows to block the intruders from getting more weapons. Evidently they know that Amphi's stunning power is gone for they no longer seem to fear getting stunned.

There are a few Pencil Heads who have the stunning power given to them by the sorceress Andrea and they are preparing to stun them. They must know now that they can stun more then one at a time after Amphi's antics last time with them. Amphi sees them pointing their skinny arms out the windows, so he quickly sends them flying back inside the room. Doing this causes them to stun several Pencil Heads who were around them. They can hear several ZZZAPS! as they approach the windows and there are a lot of Pencil Heads laying around on the floor. Amphi keeps sending the Pencil Heads back against each other and therefore keeping them off balance so they can't really do any damage. As the Pencil Heads are falling all over each other Squirt and the others are quickly cutting off their bottoms and letting them float away or tying their arms and legs together. Whenever one of those that have the stunning powers start to point at someone Amphi quickly moves their arms towards the other Pencil Heads and ZZZAP! more Pencil Heads are stunned. The CURACKS! seem to be deafening inside the room as the stuns wear off and there is nothing but mayhem ensuing as the ZZZAPS! and CURACKS! are confusing everybody. Soon though the Pencil Heads who are doing the stunning are getting their arms tied around their legs and therefore can't use the stunning powers they were given. So the powers were wasted on them and actually helped the rescuers more than hurt them.

Amphi says. "Squirt, you and Inky and a few others go to the floor below and rescue the Goddess Ameena. We'll hold them off here. Be careful though as there is a guard hiding behind the half wall as you go in. There are only two of them but more may come in while you are there, so, be quick."

"Okay!" Yells Squirt. "Come on Inky get your cousins and let's go."

"Watch out! In case the Sorceress Andrea is around. I don't know what she can do, but watch out for her in case." He yells after them. Squirt waves back at him letting him know that he heard him.

As they leave, Amphi sees Bucky and Becky go out the window with them, along with Lumina and Shiny.

He continues to toss the Pencil Heads around the room while the others are catching them and tying them up. Soon there isn't a single Pencil Head standing. Just as they are tying the last Pencil Head up, Squirt and the others are coming back through the window with the Goddess Ameena.

"Both guards were trying to see what all the zapping and the curacking was and weren't paying any attention to Goddess Ameena. We were able to untie her before they knew we were there. Then we snuck up on them and snipped off their bottoms before they could turn around." Squirt tells him.

"It was so funny. The look on their faces when we struck them." Inky says laughing. The others were all smiles too and nodding their heads in agreement.

"Quick! We have to get out of here fast because they have rigged the castle to blow up as soon as my father gets here with his army, and I don't know where the explosives are." Goddess Ameena says.

"They are getting ready to do something, but I wasn't able to learn what. I saw them bringing a lot of the statues from the garden inside the towers. The inner towers though, not the outside ones along the walls. My powers are very weak in here. As soon as I am free of the castle I will have my powers back again. So lets hurry out of the castle." She urges.

Amphi yells. "Okay let's go! Let's go back to the gate and leave through there, it is faster than through the tunnel."

With that there is a mad scramble for the windows but find that they have been covered with the same mesh as is over the castle. The sharks start to panic and try to ram their way through the mesh but are thrown back. In a mad dash they, along with some dolphins, go from window to window testing all of them. All to no avail as they are all the same and therefore just as impenetrable as all the others. The rest of the rescuers, except for Inky, Squirt, the dolphin twins and Inky's cousins Lumina and Shiny and of course Amphi, are slowly stating to panic also. They began swimming in circles and creating all kinds of bubbles and little eddies.

Amphi remembers what he was told about the mesh being impenetrable. But he also remembers that he was also told that the pencil heads could penetrate just about anything in the ocean. He tells his buddies to help quiet them down and he will get them out of there. His buddies quickly start telling the others to settle down and they will get out. They are having a hard time quieting them so Amphi starts gathering them in the middle of the room by using his power of telekinesis. Soon they are all huddled together in the middle of the room and this forces them to quiet down so Amphi can talk.

"I can get us out of here if you give me a chance." He tells them.

"Now everybody stay still for a few minutes." he says.

There is utter silence after he says this, but it is an uneasy silence and can be broken very easily at the first sign of hesitation on Amphi's part. If he shows that he's unsure of himself, panic and hysteria will take hold of everybody.

"Watch now and you'll see how easy it is to get out of here." He says confidently.

With that he quickly and expertly flings a Pencil Head head first into the mesh of the closest window. Whoosh, He goes right through it creating a huge hole. Amphi then sends more Pencil Heads through the other windows and soon they are all open again. Everybody starts cheering and began chanting;

"Amphi, Amphi, Amphi."

"Alright, Thank you, all of you. But we must get going. We have to stop King Neptune." Amphi yells.

Again there is a mad dash for the windows and this time they go through them and soon they are all headed for the first gate in a bunch. When they reach the gate they find no-one there, but the Pencil Head they had tied up when they came in. He is still laying on the ground where they left him. It is free sailing away from the castle. As soon as they are free of the castle WHAM they are all instantly transported to the old shipwreck.

"I told you my powers would return as soon as I was free. Now here we are and I can stop my father from going after the Pencil Heads." The Goddess Ameena says.

"I'll summon Link and find out where he is." she continues and waves her arms in a circular motion. Instantly Link appears as if out of nowhere.

"Where is my father?" Goddess Ameena asks him.

"Why he's about halfway to the castle by now." Link says, "He left a while ago and boy is he mad."

Goddess Ameena quickly closes her eyes in concentration as she talks with her father.

"Father!" she says, "My friends have rescued me from the Pencil Heads and I must talk to you before you reach the castle.

Please summon me and my friends to you so we can speak, and you will know I am safe."

She no sooner says this when WHAM they are all suddenly in front of King Neptune himself. He is furious and it shows on his face and in his voice.

CHAPTER 10

THE DEPARTURE

King Neptune is a big merman with snow white hair and beard on his human like face. He has fierce looking brows and even fiercer looking gray eyes that seem to spark with all the anger and wrath that he is feeling at the moment. If Amphi thought Carbs was muscular, King Neptune makes Carbs look puny with the muscular body he has. It looks like his muscles have muscles and they in turn have muscles. That's how big he looks. From the waist down though he is all fish with a tail that a whale would be proud of.

"**SPEAK DAUGHTER!!!**" He bellows. "**WHAT CAN YOU POSSIBLY SAY TO KEEP ME FROM WIPING THESE EVIL BEINGS FROM THE FACE OF THIS EARTH?**"

The force of his voice makes the water ripple and swirl about. Anyone within earshot, and that covers a lot of territory, will tremble in fright at the sound of it.

"Father, they have explosives hidden all over inside the castle and they are rigged to explode as soon as you enter the castle.

They are hoping to kill all of us at the same time." Goddess Ameena answers him calmly as though he hadn't yelled at all.

"Ah, So we are lucky that your friends have rescued you then." King Neptune says a lot more softly than he had first spoken to her and everyone breathes easier. He holds up his trident and immediately all the creatures of the deep that were with him come to a halt. Even those that are way ahead of him.

It's as though magically they all get the message at the same time. Turning towards Amphi and his friends he says:

"This must be the boy you told me about. Amphi-boy is that what you named him?"

"Yes father," Goddess Ameena says, "but it was Link who gave him that name. His name was Jamie Johnson when he was all human."

"Ugh . . . That wasn't a fit name for him down here. Link was right to change it. Amphi-boy sounds just right. And these are his friends and yours?" He asks her.

"Yes father," she answers him, "they are all my friends, but the particular group who helped save the power star with Carbs are Amphi, Squirt, and Inky. They were very helpful to Carbs in saving the power star." They all know that she wants her father to believe that Carbs was mainly the one who saved the star. They get that message when Goddess Ameena repeated that they were helpful.

"Humph!" Her father grunts, "I bet they were."

Amphi feels that he wasn't fooled and knows more than they suspect, and seeing Carbs approaching, he says:

"Here comes Carbs now."

As Carbs nears them he says.

"Hi fellas. I see you have done it again." Turning to King Neptune he says:

"King Neptune, I must confess that if it weren't for Amphi and Inky, I would probably be dead right now. They saved me from being frozen in an ice cube that the Sorceress Andrea had devised for the Pencil Heads. They and Squirt are the real heroes who saved the star and gave it to me." Carbs admits.

"I took a lot of the credit for it, hoping that you would look favorably on me. Please forgive us, your daughter and I, for trying to make you believe that I had saved the star by myself or mainly by myself." He continues.

"You think you fooled me? Or deceived me?" Says King Neptune.

"I, who knows all and sees all? You didn't fool me young Carbs, and neither did you, my dear daughter. I know how much you feel towards each other and I was hoping that eventually one of you would tell me the truth. It was very manly of you to own up to your deceit and my respect for you has risen a lot. But my daughters hand in marriage must wait a while 'till I know for a fact that something like this will never happen again."

Turning towards his daughter he says, "As for you young lady, I am very disappointed, that you thought you could deceive me. Your love for this human turned merman has interfered with your overall judgment, and that is why your cousin was able to get the best of you. I hope you have learned a valuable lesson here." Turning to Amphi, he says:

"I know of all that you have been doing since my daughter saved you from drowning. Link has kept me informed of your deeds, and I have seen some of them myself in my minds eye.

You have indeed been deserving of her saving your life and I do not fault her for doing that. You are using your powers that you were granted wisely even though they were given to you for the main purpose of helping these two lovers to get together. I therefore am restoring the stun power back to you and am going to allow you to keep the powers you have been given as long as you use them for good and not for evil, like Ameena's cousin is doing. You also have other powers that you are not aware of yet.

You will eventually learn them and how to control them in time.

You may even discover them for yourself if the occasion arises. Hopefully that won't happen. Not to soon anyway. I will have to deal with Andrea eventually, but for now I can't interfere with what is going on. I have to let matters solve themselves for reasons I am not at liberty to say at this time." With that he touches Amphi on the shoulder with his trident, and says:

"What I declare and give out cannot be taken away by anyone but me, and I declare that the powers you now possess shall always be yours until I take them away."

When he finishes saying this, Amphi feels a jolt, like an electric shock go through his whole body.

"I have also granted you the ability to see through objects as far as you want. This is the reward you get for being faithful to my daughter and for being the brains behind saving her. Now tell me, what would you do right now about the Pencil Heads?"

King Neptune asks him.

"Well, I know that if you have granted me the power to see though things, than you most certainly can also see through things and therefore when we go to the castle you, and I now, will be able to see where the explosives are that they have placed hoping to kill us and we can take them out. After we remove them, then we can capture the Pencil Heads and you will dispose of them as you see fit."

"A very wise and intelligent answer. My daughter was right in saving your life for you have a gift for solving difficult situations. That is exactly what we will do. Let's continue on to the castle but do not enter it. We will surround it and be prepared to enter all at once after we remove the explosives." King Neptune says.

"Let us proceed now to the castle but be alert for anything for they know we are coming."

Raising his trident once again they all continue on their journey to the castle. Remember it is quite a ways away still. On the way there Amphi practices his ability to see through things by looking at everything that is solid. He sees a barrel that evidently fell off a boat long ago and he can see that it is empty except for a moray eel that is using it for a hiding place. He is surprised as to how clearly he can see the eel. Looking at the barrel normally, he doesn't see the eel at all, but turning on his ex-ray vision, as he calls it, he can see the eel clearly. He steers everybody away from the barrel without telling them what's inside. As a whale come close, he can see a couple of tires in the whales belly and it makes him smile. The female whale that is swimming beside him is pregnant and Amphi can see the tiny baby inside her. He thinks this is amazing. Evidently King Neptune can see what he sees for suddenly he hears him in his head say:

"You must remember to respect every ones privacy and not invade it or intrude on their private things. You must not reveal whatever you see that is private. Keep that in mind always."

Amphi immediately stops looking at the baby and replies:

"Yes sir. I didn't realize she was pregnant 'till I looked and it was beautiful to see the baby. I have never seen such a thing before and I would never do anything to hurt them. I will be more careful from now on."

"Okay." says King Neptune, "Let's continue on."

It isn't very much longer and they are approaching the castle, or what is left of it. As they come near they see all the towers suddenly rising up off the bottom and what looks like flames coming out of the bottom of the towers. Amphi knows right away what they are and he quickly tells King Neptune that they must stop or be burned alive. These are space ships that are lifting off and they will be throwing off a lot of heat.

King Neptune raises his trident and all the creatures of the deep start swimming swiftly back away from them. They swim back a safe distance and turn to watch. There is a lot of dirt and rocks and shells being thrown up by the blast of the ships rising. They are rising fast and Amphi and the others are following them upwards. As they rise higher they can see them clearer as the water isn't disturbed here. They can see the Pencil Heads looking out the windows of the 'towers' turned space ships. They soon reach the surface and continue up into the night sky and they suddenly step on the gas because they are very soon disappearing from sight.

All of the sea creatures that followed Amphi to the surface, now begin to go back down to the bottom. The sand is settling back down and King Neptune has commanded the waters to quiet down and not make waves. As soon as the bottom is quiet again, King Neptune instructs the others to wait while he and Amphi check out the grounds inside the walls or what's left of them anyway. The two of them venture into what used to be the castle. There is just a few walls still standing, but most of the walls were destroyed by the ships taking off and a few of the wall towers are still standing.

On the outside of one of the walls they find the guard that Amphi and his friends had tied up before. Nobody ever found him and he was still there where they had left him. He was badly burned and barely alive with no arms or legs for they had been burned off.

King Neptune asked the Pencil Head what had happened.

Why were they leaving?

The Pencil Head says, "The council was not happy with how everything is turning out and they took a vote." The Pencil Head gasps. He's talking very low and breathing hard.

"They decided that this planet is too harsh and violent for us to stay here. They thought we could take over this planet and make it our own, seeing as ours was dying, but there are too many different beings here. Even the surface dwellers are violent and defensive of their planet. We are only an advance force to find out if we can survive here. They voted to go and find a more suitable planet to live on . . . . We cannot survive here." He gasped out this last part just before closing his eyes in death.

Looking around, King Neptune sees only bits and pieces left of what was once a mighty castle. He and Amphi swim along the ground not daring to touch it for fear that there may be an explosive device buried. After checking all around and inside the remaining towers and under them they discover that there are no explosives. Either the Pencil Heads had decided not to booby trap the place or the rockets had set off the explosives, and that's probably why there were only bits and pieces left of the walls and towers.

Amphi calls King Neptune's attention to what remains of the garden. Upon examining the statues that are left, King Neptune decides that none of the statues would be worth saving for they were all damaged to some extent by the rockets and if they were revived to life again they would be crippled so badly that they would probably wish they had never been saved. They were actually too far gone to be saved with decency, so therefore King Neptune ordered all the sea creatures to back off a ways. When all were clear of the remains of the castle, King Neptune, with a wave of his trident, quickly created a huge hole in the floor of the ocean and buried all the statues. Then he piled a ton of rocks on top to mark their grave. With that he said: "May they forever rest in peace."

He then orders the creatures of the deep to scatter and proceed with their lives, for all is over and there is no longer any threat.

With a wave of his trident, the trio, Amphi, Squirt and Inky, suddenly find themselves back at the shipwreck from where they started.

In Amphi's head he hears King Neptune say, "We will keep in touch and I will let you know when I need you. You and your friends have fun and enjoy yourselves."

So ends the problem of the Pencil Heads.

THE END

ABOUT THE AUTHOR

Herbert Victor Fernandes Sr. is a 69 year old 218 pound man, who lives with his wife of 45 years in Arcadia, Florida. Her name is Sharon and was a big help in his writing of this, his very first attempt at writing. She read and reread the story as it was unfolding and made several valuable, important, contributions to the story. He worked for many years as a welder in construction helping to erect power plants and feed mills and grain elevators in Connecticut and Arkansas. Worked for Electric Boat out of Connecticut welding on submarines for the Navy. Where he broke his back in 1973 and had a spinal fusion of the 4th,5th and #1 sacral discs. He also operated a back hoe and a 10 ton crane called a cherry picker in the construction field.

After retiring from the construction field, and after several hernia operations from lifting steel beams and such, he worked for 10 years for the Brunswick Recreation Centers and became an assistant manager with them. He retired in 1997 due to having triple bypass surgery and crushing his heel by falling off a ladder. He's no spring chicken and has led a pretty hard life. Having gone under the knife nine times for different operations. He and his wife have raised three wonderful children, 2 boys and a girl, who are all married and raising families of their own now. He has three grandsons and one granddaughter.